The Tower of Glass

Ivan Ângelo

Translation by Ellen Watson

Dalkey Archive Press

For Mariana and Camila
my daughters

Library of Congress Cataloging-in-Publication Data

Ângelo, Ivan, 1936-
    [Casa de vidro. English]
    The tower of glass / Ivan Ângelo ; translation by Ellen Watson.— 1st Dalkey Archive ed.
        p. cm.
    ISBN 1-56478-346-4 (alk. paper)
        I. Title.

    PQ9698.1.N474C3713 2004
    869.3'42—dc22
                                                            2003070089

Partially funded by grants from the National Endowment for the Arts, a federal agency,
and the Illinois Arts Council, a state agency.

Dalkey Archive books are published by the Center for Book Culture, a nonprofit organization
located at Milner Library, Illinois State University.

www.centerforbookculture.org

Printed on permanent / durable acid-free paper and bound in the United States of America.

Praise for Ivan Ângelo

"The depths of Brazilian society are captured in five interconnected stories that expose the horror, turmoil, and poverty of people who struggle for survival and against oppression. . . . Ângelo's pungent vignettes reveal with unflinching revulsion all the despair, passion, and anguish that this situation has created."

—*Booklist*

"Ângelo presents his events and characters through a variety of techniques and styles, like a juggler showing all his tricks."

—*Washington Post*

"Ivan Ângelo is one of the best fiction writers in Brazil today."
—Galeno de Freitas, translator of Eduardo H. Galeano

"*The Celebration* is a portrait, a kaleidoscope, an assembly, a masterpiece."

—Assis Brasil

CONTENTS

CONQUEST

"and those who producd more than an agreed upon quantitie were payd as rewarde one vintem eache day, and hence the more pleasant and productive they became. The kitchen negresses, when not occupyd with theyr pots of marmelade and other famous concoctions wich were exported by mule to Rio de Janeyro, gave themselves to the courtesys of the eight men of the hous, wich is how many we numberd, and earnd one vintem eache for the goode they accorded us."

(Estevam de Saa Perdigão—Commemorative of the Discoverie of Lost Golde.)

Here we have Mr. Omar Pires de Moura, talented executive, back at the office. Take note: though exhibiting apparent interest and unapproachable superiority he is barely tolerating yet another early-morning meeting of management to consider possible responses to the striking workers. His department has prepared a careful survey rendering useless all the tedious theories of those mongoloids who make it their business to worry about politics, including a list of all the imponderable circumstances which could influence this or that and, suddenly fed up with it all, here we have the prestigious and loudmouthed financial wiz speaking out of turn and putting an end to that idiotic and pointless discussion, by analyzing the company's production over the last five years as it relates to national production and the exigencies of the economic sector, establishing once and for all, beyond a shadow of a doubt, the irreversible necessities, outlining a reassuring profile of the firm's prospective performance regardless of the political course of the nation as a whole, skillfully demonstrating the necessity of a purely technical approach to the question, examining the production chart along with the other department heads who are utterly fascinated and submissive to his talent and persuasiveness, and here he is, at last, proclaiming that they should be able to absorb, without risk, a salary hike of up to thirty percent, then finally volunteering to deliver personally to the workers the calculations proving that due to a and b their pay raise can be no greater than fifteen percent. Ha, ha, ha, here he is returning to his desk, to Elza his secretary, who unquestionably thinks he looks like Omar

3

Sharif but of course says nothing, adoring, as he explains how the report should be set up and why it is of the utmost urgency, but then, at the sight of her carefully manicured hands, he turns into the profligate Sir Henry Spencer Ashbee, dreaming about how those red fingernails could just as well be caressing his skillful two-by-eight instead of having to type all night preparing that report with accompanying statement of terms and proposal to the strikers.

Next we have the legendary British libertine Sir Henry Spencer Ashbee on his way to the club to meet his friend and brother-in-law, Sir Harold, following yet another delectable adventure in which his famous two-by-eight once again played the gusty role of king of the muff-snatchers. All of Sir Henry's considerable finesse and aplomb will be necessary at this encounter to ensure that he doesn't lose his temper and end up slapping Sir Harold in the face for his persistent expressions of disbelief—often without so much as the delicacy to check who is at the neighboring tables or use an appropriately discreet tone of voice—with regard to his lascivious activities. Sir Henry, not a man of great patience, has in the past managed to restrain himself only because Sir Harold knows of all his intrigues and is, as it were, brother to his fortune; but if things reach an unbearable limit today, as they have several times previously—today of all days, a day filled with general irritation at the office due to the strike in the Osasco factory which already has him out of sorts, and then afterward there was that abominable traffic tie-up caused by a minor collision which prompted two cretins to discuss at great length the issue of who would pay to have their cars repainted while all Rua Augusta yelled and honked, obliging the irritated Sir Henry to abandon his car in a no-parking zone and seek refuge in a massage parlor, with delicious consequences; if, then, irony and suspicion are forthcoming from Sir Harold, Sir Henry, somewhat relieved from having taken his pleasure but nonetheless undermined by cumulative irritation, will be obliged to forget kinship and expedience and come out swinging. Here, then, we have the notorious adventurer striding into the bar, drawing reproachful glances from the family men, surmising their whispered remarks: Here he comes again, the fornicating philanderer. Inaccessible, with an air of contempt for the values of that lazy bourgeoisie, he twists his mustache between thumb and forefinger, smoothing any hairs which might be out of place, a characteristic gesture, and scans the room for Sir Harold. With a measured, decisive, and, as much as possible, sensual stride, he advances toward his friend's table after an almost invisible gesture of greeting—such exemplary British discretion. Listen now as Sir Henry recounts at length for the friend of his youth, companion in some of the most outrageous revels in all São Paulo, long before becoming his brother-in-law, godfather to his son, and accomplice, listen as he recounts his ingenious, tortuous maneuverings to corrupt the reluctant masseuse. There are other girls for that, she had said to Sir Henry the Dangerous, as he reported to Sir Harold, you can ask for one who does, he quoted her, trying his best to convey her sensual manner in order to give Sir Harold an approximate picture of what a hot number she was, supplying his friend with the raw material to evaluate the diabolical offer he made her even though she was a relatively upright young woman, with a daughter, who swore she worked there only because she really, really had to. At the sauna she earned six thousand before tips; in a store on Rua Augusta she would have only made two thousand. I want my daughter to have everything, the very best, she said, and Sir Henry was emphatic in his narrative, painting the scene like an artist, until finally he came to the conclusion, the irresistable offer of two thousand cruzeiros, and her tears as she yielded, giving in to everything. Every little thing. A blonde?—Sir Harold inquired, perhaps with a certain air of incredulity, or maybe irritating superiority, the satyr wasn't quite sure how to define it, and so he revealed, as proof, that the girl was a blonde with black pubes, like Marilyn Monroe.

(

—It's my greatest frustration.

—I know, it's tough, they're so rare in Brazil. Except in the South.

—Well, they could bleach it all, at the same time.

—God forbid. Then we'd never know for sure. I'd rather see the stamp, right there, plain as day: codfish from Norway.

—Not me. Phony, genuine, dark beer, light beer, bone-in, boneless, filet, chuck steak, it's all the same to me. I just give it the old one-two.

—You'd think you had the biggest appetite in town!

—Well, I *am* the hungry type.

—Sure you are. I've seen you in action.

—What are you talking about? Seen what?

—Get a few whiskeys in you and *shhhlump*, you're out of it. You couldn't see the feast if she were right in front of you. Or else it's slam-bam-thank-you-ma'am.

—Of course *you're* the champion, you're the know-it-all.

—That's right. All modesty aside, I do know it all.

—You don't know anything. Tais told me all about you.

—You're kidding.

—I'm serious.

—Women. They're obsessed with talking about men. So-and-so's got such a tiny little pecker, they're all faggots. Every one of them's got a pet complaint. All they do is talk.

—Not with me. With me it's the good old one-two.

—They're just trying to prove they screw more than we do. They think it's their turn to take the initiative.

—Sure, because guys like you keep making up stories.

(The waiter leaves two more drafts and two shotglasses of Steinhegen on the table.)

—Whoever calls the shots in bed calls the shots in life, that's what I say.

—The other day I was with one who tried to stick her finger up my ass.

—You're not serious.

—No shit. Right at the last minute, there she is with her finger.

—Just what we need.

)

Here we have the famous race-car driver maneuvering his super-machine with understated dexterity, indifferent to all the adoring looks from those he passes. There he goes taking a dangerous curve alongside a killer bus, a bus gone mad, bent on eliminating successful industrialists. With precise movements the eminent champion downshifts to second gear, floors it, tires shrieking, and escapes by a slim quarter of an inch the monstrous vehicle closing in on him, as the frustrated bus driver is rewarded with the sound of the racer's horn bleating the terrible song of winners. Now the ace competitor must battle the stopwatch, shaving off seconds as he weaves through traffic, taking shortcuts down one-way streets, because he's supposed to be home by five o'clock and at the airport by five twenty, and he lost a good half hour trying to get a hitchhiker to fondle his agitated organ. And here is the fearless champion receiving the flag at exactly five o'clock, not a second late, the hitchhiker's address stashed away in his wallet, you never know . . .

And now we have the dutiful husband, master in the art of cynicism, arriving home pissed off, complaining about the traffic, which is why he couldn't get there sooner, in time for a real good-bye. Take note: the rascal pats the soon-to-be traveler's flabby poopdeck to demonstrate exactly what he means by a real good-bye, and she smiles, lamenting the *forza del destino*, what can you do. Here he is in the car again, the cautious driver on the way to the airport with his precious cargo. He listens once more to the whole story of his mother-in-law's impending operation, they suspect cancer, and never tires of repeating: If you need me just call, I'll get there as soon as I can. I'll drop everything, the factory, the strike, and come. He knows how to convey the security that comes from a husband who is there for her, in solidarity; he drives with an air of unhurried precision, glancing at her, a woman neither ugly nor pretty, dressed with the kind of good taste that doesn't show, the modest disguise of a woman who is incessantly demanding in bed. Now observe the perfect husband as he gets out of the car and summons a redcap with just the fingers of his right hand, no broad, vulgar gestures for him, the distinguished gentleman accompanied by his wife, and observe how he stifles the expression of relief and freedom he's beginning to feel a trifle ahead of time. Refined as he is, he doesn't make mistakes, he doesn't stare, for example, at that strange blonde walking by with her midriff showing—a guy in drag?—and instead insists one more time that she telephone as soon as the surgery is over. He knows how to pretend that he's listening to her, the cunning fellow, when actually he's thinking what is it with that damned plane, why haven't they called the flight yet, and therefore he's unaware that he's promised, with an affirmative nod of the head in answer to a buzzing of questions, he's promised not to let the girls stay out late and not to let Cacaio ride his motorcycle without telling him where he's going. Perfect, utterly perfect, the shameless dissembler makes believe he doesn't even hear the loudspeakers announcing the flight of freedom, the anxiety should be hers not his, and just as he was rehearsing a casual question like "Isn't that your flight?" she finally hears the second call, and is last in line, taken by surprise when he kisses her, on the mouth—ah, perfect scoundrel—and she turns, still troubled, from the other side of the glass, to see him say, "Call me!" cranking his hand in circles next to his ear, his mouth forming the soundless words and finally a last wave good-bye, she's on her way to the deathbed. As he turns around, poof, he's Sir Henry Spencer Ashbee in person.

Here we have the dangerous despoiler chasing after your daughters down busy commercial streets in late afternoon. His eyes are serpents' tongues licking their arms, their cleavage; he is poison. His hands fondle posteriors from afar. Observe: his prey! Observe Sir Henry Spencer Ashbee on the scent of his prey, he's a panther slinking between clumps of people, eyes fixed on the desired flesh, observe his feline posture before the lunge, he draws abreast of the victim, a nervous gazelle just now sensing the danger, the smell, the telltale crackling sound behind her; the appetizing morsel freezes, and crunch, he attacks. I'd love to, but, well, not just now, a previous appointment, some other time perhaps, but unfortunately, well, who knows, it's been a pleasure, *ciao*. Observe with what urbanity Sir Henry takes his leave, enchanting her with the possibility of a future encounter, and observe how his philandering eyes and in fact his whole body fortify themselves anew for the quest for a juicier little dove, as he wheels in circles through shop clerks, bank tellers, bookkeepers, secretaries. Only those corrupt eyes know how to scan the plain for the sudden movement of those who have already given up on marriage, those who would be willing to risk a flight of adventure. Observe the rapscallion as he soars close to his prey, herding her from the flock, making a show of his dangerous and elegant glide, and jingling his car keys so she'll know in advance that what awaits her is a marvelous jaunt, far from the repetitive bus window, a ride on the wings of the wind. Sir Henry knows it won't do to attack a frightened bird too precipitously, he knows there's a certain rhythm to it, a crescendo, but overexcited by his recent freedom— shit, the sky belongs to the condor!—he blurts, "I'm going to bite you all over," clearly a mistake since she had merely accepted an invitation for a drink or two, and so that was the end of that: she backed away, suddenly remembering an appointment, and his offer of five hundred, a thousand cruzeiros only made things worse. The dove flitted off into the crowd. And there he goes again, invincible, undressing every one of them with his sharp eyes. There's the scoundrel sauntering along next to a lovely set of breasts who fail to return his interest, fail to stop when he murmurs, "Listen, I'd really like to talk to you"; on the contrary, the girl quickens her step, and the wicked Sir Henry delights in the voluptuous movement of her ass, while at the same time he searches for other bodies in the throng which, by now, is thinning. He mentally fondles that fundament as he follows her through the crowd to the corner where he pretends to be interested in a set of luggage in the window, but it's just a pause before retracing his steps, a pause so people who saw him go after her won't see him returning without his trophy, and then a woman appears, the kind of woman who stops at store windows to give her pursuer an opening, a woman almost his age, hunting as he is, and they recognize each other as animals of the same species, almost smile without looking at each other, aware of each other's presence, as if to say, "If only you were twenty years younger," and the distinguished Sir Henry Spencer Ashbee withdraws, leaving the field in front of the window of suitcases open for her, and as he departs he catches a glimpse of a pair of blue slacks approaching her furtively. The notorious ravisher, slightly disturbed by now that the streets seem to be emptying before he has managed to procure adequate nourishment for his voracious two-by-eight, crosses the Plaza João Mendes and scans the lines of people waiting for buses, searching for some tired working girl to whom a hot bath and scrumptious one-night stand would seem more alluring than the hour-and-a-half bus trip home to the suburbs where later that evening some modest bank clerk would paw her still-beautiful breasts and place in her hands, or inside her, a tool which would award her no other satisfaction than a few moans. Ah, this ruffian feels like staging a demonstration on top of a park bench to persuade them, he'd flash his money, flaunt his marvelous member, and lead them all astray, a long line of women filling his afternoons for years and years. The experienced enticer knows it's no easy task to lure fair maidens from their place in line, won after such a long wait, but he has had previous success in this delicate maneuver. Observe how he operates, the rascal: standing in a neutral spot near the tail end of two or three lines, he exercises his technique, alert to each person getting in line yet at the same time so very casual, as if waiting for someone, masterfully camouflaging his intentions. Here we have the marvelous charlatan suddenly advancing toward the middle line, swiftly, so that no one can beat him to the spot right behind that succulent little brunette who speaks directly to the necessities of his muff-raker. The technique developed by Sir Henry demands that he wait until a bus arrives, the line lengthening behind him, before he begins a more frontal attack; by then she will have moved up toward the middle of the line, a candidate for standing room on the next bus or a seat on the following one, and thus would be unlikely to run off and forfeit her place. The only danger is that if two buses arrive at once there will be no time for polite conversation. At this initial point of contact, though, he need only be his refined and elegant self, leaning close enough for her to detect the scent of the interested male animal as well as the fragrance of a scrupulously clean man, and yet remain distant enough so that she will take no offense or, worse, confuse him with a simple accoster. This is also the time to show his most attractive facial angle, which in Sir Henry's case is the right profile, so that she may surreptitiously steal a look at the source of all that disturbing male heat. Ah, now she knows he's handsome, sexy, and interested. What more could a salesgirl ask for in late afternoon after at least eight hours waiting on people or stuck behind a cash register? Emboldened by these thoughts and fearing the arrival of two buses simultaneously, he commences his unsettling attack with the elegance of a toreador, chatting about the delay. He senses that things are falling into place when she responds in the same casual tone, remarking that it's typical, totally disorganized, an interminable wait and then two or three arrive together, and the tore-ador knows that luck is on his side *en la plaza* today, imagine if he had left conversation for later and two buses *had* come at once. Four or five minutes of exhibition in the arena and he's ready to take out his car keys, as if distractedly, and in a few more minutes he'll mention that he's tak-ing the bus because he's going to such-and-such an address and doesn't know the neighborhood, it's so hard these days to get a cab. And then, the first pair of *banderillas*, he announces his car is nearby in a parking garage. More talk about the neighborhood, more *banderillas* as he ques-tions her about the obvious streets she knows so well but with which he—*olé!*—is unfamiliar since he's new in town. The well-rehearsed rogue chooses with the skill of a matador the moment for the thrust, the invitation, the courtesy she would do him to accompany him by car and show him the way and—*olé!*—she succumbs. Now, in the car, here we have the despoiler, defiler, big-time operator, trying to dissuade his reluctant conquest from going home, and being informed that she has another job, she needs to take a shower, change her clothes, rest for ten minutes, and be at work at nine. She allows his hand to wander up her leg to just a little above the knee, feeling the flesh under the thin fabric of her slacks, but no farther, sufficient motivation to arouse his pulsing two-by-eight which she declines to touch when Sir Henry guides her hand toward the spot, the hand which had been until that moment resting casually on his leg, experienced girl that she is. She seems to relax visibly, irritating this impatient muff-lubricator somewhat, and explains, completely unruffled, that she will only be able to go out with him at one o'clock, first she has to dance for four hours as a go-go girl at the Executive Bar. You can't see it in his face, but the indefatigable horizontalist is a little disappointed to hear about her second profession, since it probably explains why things have gone so smoothly, and a good deal more disappointed about the delay, but she says there's no way she can miss work, she's already been out twice this week, God help me if I lose this job. As they say good-bye he complains, "Shit, honey, you work so hard," no longer feeling the need to make a point of his right profile, thinking about stopping off at the bar for a chat with Sir Harold. Just look at the nerve this lecher has, charging her for the ride: a slow caress of the bush beneath her slacks before she gets out of the car—look at him get her to promise that this will be a historic night for his two-by-eight, guiding her now docile hand to just the right spot, a pleasure to meet you Elisabete, Bete.

Now here's the lucky fellow in the bar tormenting the life out of Sir Harold with the prospect of a delirious night with Miss Elizabeth, the famous ballerina, as he guzzles whiskey and munches french fries. Sir Harold is concerned about his mother's surgery but can't seem to manage to worry his brother-in-law, who sees in her hospitalization more the good of freedom than the evil of cancer: It's nothing, you'll see. They take turns fiercely impaling french fries and checking the room for women, teeth gnashing, as they ready their party-picks for another stab at the hot golden pulp. Sir Henry is perhaps drinking more than he should, since it's only ten o'clock and he has three more hours to wait before the rendezvous with his lady friend. Cautioned by his accomplice he protests, in a tone a bit less than refined, there's not a person who can say he's missed a single day because of drinking! Suddenly—maybe a familiar-looking dress, or someone with freckles—the chief executive remembers Elza, his secretary, and the report for tomorrow *without fail*. He decides to call her, but gives up when he finds the phone at the bar occupied, thinking it's all right, she'll manage. Not a bad idea to give her a good banging one of these days, Sir Henry thinks, returning to the table, and he mentions to Sir Harold that just the other day he was explaining to Cacaio how different it was, how hard it was, to get a woman in the old days,

(

—First you had to get to know the family. A girl who went out with boys alone, or gallivanted around by herself, was definitely not the kind to marry. That kind was only for messing around. A good girl, once she agreed to go together, after a little flirting—staring at each other from a distance, that's what we called flirting—would take you to meet the family. That was the start of the romance.

—And then you could kiss and stuff, right?

—Are you kidding? Not a chance, my boy. First you had to eat a lot of cookies and drink coffee in the living room, you couldn't even hold her hand. This phase lasted a long time.

—Did you watch TV?

—TV? In those days television wasn't what it is today, hardly anybody had one, only the very rich. The romance was all in the talking. As for going out, well, you could go to the movies but you had to bring a brother or sister as chaperone. Or if you wanted to go to a party, to dance, someone had to come along, too. A couple was only allowed out alone after gaining the parents' trust, which took months. And even then, going out in that atmosphere of watchfulness, the Holy Spirit watching everything from up above, well, there was a certain suspense just in holding the girl's hand. Putting your arm around her, around the back of her seat at the movies, whew, that was a battle. You'd put it there, she'd take it away, you'd put it back, she'd leave it there for a little while, then she'd think you were letting it drift down too far and she'd push it away again. And a kiss, a kiss was a real kiss. But we were a movie generation, we courted like in the movies. We copied the way they kissed, the hairstyles, the clothes, the way they talked. I learned more at the movies than I ever did in school.

—And what did you do after the movie?

—Well, they knew exactly how long it took to get home, of course, the movie house was right in the neighborhood, and going downtown was only for when you were engaged or chaperoned. But there was always time for a little hugging. Gradually the intimacy grew, it had a kind of sequence to it, each day some small new thing, a few steps backward, then a step forward, until—well. That took months, in the most serious cases, years.

—So the thing to do was to get married.

—Right. From there on out you had to get married.

—And that's what it was like with Mother?

—With everyone. It was the same for anyone my age, anyone over forty. That's what the world was like.

—What a bunch of shit, huh?

—Hey, a little respect . . .

)

how many techniques a man had to develop which—it turns out—nowadays women find a lot more charming than the young pups. That's for sure, says Sir Harold with a belch, and they go on and on—what a job it was just to get a good feel, or to get permission to shelter your little bird in the nest between two thighs—leisurely peopling the prospective evening with the ever-present emotions of adolescence.

(

—I don't think they do that anymore, tuck it in between thighs.

—Nah, that's something from our day, remember: aw, come on, *please*, not even a little snuggle between thighs?

—Yeah, that was the line all right.

—That's what I was telling my son the other day. We made our conquests piece by piece.

—With a battle for each piece.

—You bet. After a given area was conquered, though, it meant permanent access. It was like a right.

—And that was the last stop, between the thighs.

—Good thing it was so good, huh?

—God yes.

—We didn't really want it to go further than that, any more than they did, all hell might break loose. All that mad rubbing back and forth, one-two, one-two . . .

—Or else you could put it in the back door.

—Hardly.

—People do it.

—Not me.

—Well, not me either, but people did. Remember that old saying: She's only a virgin up front?

—Sure, but . . . I don't know, it's just not for me. What I liked was the slow progression, the . . . game of it, that's what it was, a game, don't you think? Each time we conquered a new piece of ground we were beside ourselves, bursting with happiness, we'd laugh all the way home, remembering every detail.

—How sweet it was.

—That's for sure.

(Now the men are nibbling on hot dogs, spearing more french fries.)

—There was a sort of code, remember? All those little signals. It was subtle, nonverbal. When a girl wore a straight skirt you knew from the start there'd be trouble: no thigh business at all, am I right? A wide skirt was a sign it was okay. If she wore a blouse with no opening, forget it. If it closed up the back: we'll see, could go either way. But a blouse with buttons down the front, all right! Full steam ahead. Fan-tastic.

—And remember those dresses with zippers down the side?

—"Mama's coming." That's what they were called. If you heard her mother coming all you had to do was: ZIP!

—Fan-tastic. And at the movies . . . you could put your right arm behind her on the seat while the left worked the zipper down below.

—Wait a minute, wasn't it the other way around?

—No, how could you forget? The zipper was on this side, like so, from here to here. It was the left side, I'm sure of it.

—I'm not sure, details like that . . .

—It was the left, I'm positive. So much simpler than all that business of getting up under the skirt. Perfectly discreet.

—Made for it.

—Of course it was. The guy's body shielded the side with the zipper, his hand went inside, the two heads huddled together, and all you could hear was that long gasping noise, her half-opened lips sucking air in slowly, so as not to make a lot of noise, like this: *shshshshshshshsh* —then a pause, almost a sigh, as she let out the air, then another *shshshshshshshshsh*, real soft.

—God, it was good, wasn't it . . .

(Both men inhale slowly, enjoying the smell of cheese on their fingers, then recognize the same gesture in the other, a moment of identification.)

—Any girl who got engaged and didn't end up marrying the guy was in trouble.

—Practically impossible to find anyone else.

—Sure, everybody figured someone had already been there. I wonder how women feel about those days, you know?

—I bet they get mad just thinking about it. About all they missed.

—What about all we missed?

—We didn't miss anything. For us there was always the Zone, or a little roll in the hay with the maid. We didn't miss much.

—Our generation got stuck in the middle, though. When we were young we couldn't do anything. Of course now that I've hit forty the girls today can do anything they like, you know what I mean? That's what we missed out on—the young ones.

—Ah, you're right about that.

—Though I must say I got off a few good ones in my time.

—Yeah, me too. Paying homage to Maria de Fátima, Maria Eugênia, Olga. Every last one of them.

—What energy we had!

—You said it! There were days I had an even dozen.

—A dozen?

—Mmmmm. 'Course by the end there was nothing left. It hurt like crazy and there I was.

—I maybe made eight, max. Counting the whole day, I mean.

—Sure, the whole day. Starting in the morning at school, then came lunch, and a two-hour wait for digestion, and then things picked up again later in the little room, sort of a closet, under the back stairs— that's where I kept my magazines—and on and on until bedtime.

—The minimum was three.

(One sucks his slender cigarette, the other his fat cigar, ah—what pleasure.)

—I started when I was ten, eleven years old.

—Me too, around there, ten or eleven.

—Before eleven, I think. Ha, I remember banging the banana tree, did you do that?

—Nah, we didn't have one. We used to ram the ravine, though. Just dig a little hole in the soft dirt and go at it.

—Ram the ravine, now that's one I never tried.

—It scrapes a little.

—Banana trees are pretty good. We had a couple of them at the country place, we used to make a hole in the trunk, you could sort of embrace it, even, just like a person. And get this—there's this sticky stuff that would ooze out, out of the hole. The problem was the way it stained, you couldn't get it off your clothes. Our mother was always giving us trouble, wanting to know where we got those impossible stains.

—Of course the regulation method was just plain spit.

—Yeah, right. Sometimes you could be inventive, but only when you had time and space.

—I used to use different things for lubrication. Now and then.

—Now and then. The basics were just spit, cock, and hand.

—Know what I used? My mother's Rugol. It was some kind of skin cream, remember?

—Sure. I think I tried something like that too. But you had to be careful they didn't notice it was getting used up.

—Right. Just a little bit now and then.

—I could take it or leave it. But coconut fat, now that's something. Carioca Coconut Fat.

—Or lard.

—Without salt. The kind with salt burned like hell.

—Bacon fat.

—Butter.

—Cooking oil.

—Baby oil.

—Sewing maching oil.

—Soap.

—Except it hurt like a son-of-a-bitch.

—Yeah, soap was for shit.

—Vaseline.

—You had Vaseline at your house? What for?

—Sure, didn't you?

—In your parents' bedroom?

—No, in the bathroom.

—And every once in a while it spent the night in your parents' room, right?

—I don't know, I never noticed.

—Then what did they buy it for?

—We put it on our hair.

—We used brilliantine, not Vaseline.

—My mother couldn't stand the smell of brilliantine. Royal Briar, Glostora, Colgate, she thought all of them were awful. I didn't really like them either, guess I got it from her.

—Didn't like them where? On your dipstick?

—On my hair. Such a strong smell.

—What about on your dipstick?

—No, not there either, I don't think. 'Cause of the smell.

—I liked it okay.

—The rate you go you must have used a bottle a week.

—Well, you had to vary it, so no one would notice. Besides, I only used stuff like that when I knew nobody was around. It was a real job to clean up afterward.

—You know how I liked it? Stomach down, rubbing on the bed.

—That's the best way in the morning. You could also do it in the shower, soap up your hands and lean them against the wall like this, like a tube, and just move your hips. You ever do it like that?

—I did it every way there was. Some people make up all kinds of stories, though, you can't believe a word of it. Like that business of lying in a bathtub full of water with just the head sticking out, and you set a fly with no wings on the tip, for a "stroll around the island"—who's got time to go hunting flies and all that?!

—In the movies we just rubbed back and forth on top of our clothes. Simple. Sometimes a couple times per movie.

—Or else you could make a hole in your pants pocket.

—They sewed it up, we ripped it open again.

—A war.

—Once in a while I'd get off just walking down the street.

—Me too, plenty of times.

—What a life, eh?

—Crazy. And think of the number of women we "paid our respects to" over the years.

—Good God.

—I even screwed Nioka, the comic book character, that way.

—Me too.

—And Jane, Tarzan's Jane.

—Sure. The movie, and the comic book version too. But the really hot one in the comics was Sheena, remember her?

—Sheena?

—The blonde with wild hair. Her clothes were all tattered, made of tiger pelts or something. Showed a lot of skin, anyway. I nailed her a bunch of times.

—Not me. Not that one. But what about L'il Abner's girlfriend?

—Se-e-ex-x-y. And that other one, Prudence Pimpleton? Sex on wheels.

(There's a pause in the men's conversation, and each of them lovingly fondles his dark bottle of beer, playing with the label, thinking, remembering. Then something is said and the silence is broken.)

—Now, one woman I had a long-term affair with was Luz del Fuego, remember that picture that came out in O Cruzeiro when she was thrown out of the Municipal Carnival Ball wearing an outfit consisting of nothing but a snake? Did you see it?

—Eve from Paradise. That was the name of her costume. I got real friendly with that photo too.

—Remember the movie Carnival on Fire? I saw it five times. And made it with a different girl each day. There was Elvira Paga singing "I saw a bull in España, and what a bull, Mr. Peçaña"—unbelievable. She was almost completely naked.

—And there was Cuquita Carballo dancing the rhumba, her ass coming right out of the screen onto our cocks.

—And the Parisi sisters, they were real bombshells, remember? I saw them in the theater, too, a matinee. Now that was money well spent, I'll tell you. Couldn't decide which to look at, I was madly in love with both of them. Fourteen years old, real passion. I almost ran away, I wanted to follow them back to Rio.

(The waiter's hurried hands bring two more phalluses of beer and two shotglasses dripping with Steinhegen. The men stroke their glasses tenderly and then toss the contents down their avid throats.)

—I had a whole scrapbook of movie stars. I guess everybody did.

—You bet. This thick.

—With the same collection probably. Me here, in São Paulo, and you down in Porto Alegre, the same damn collection.

—Exactly. For instance: I didn't have a single picture from a Brazilian movie in mine.

—Of course not! Just that one of Luz del Fuego, that's all.

—Domestic features were so routine, plain beans and rice. No one wanted local stuff.

—How could it compare to those fantastic blondes in the movies?

—Those perfect teeth.

—Their hair, the way they walked, their clothes. Perfection. Not one with crooked teeth, clothes that hung wrong, scuffed shoes. And those voices—sultry, sexy, not like the cracked bamboo from down here.

—It's their teeth that drive me wild. A different race altogether.

—I was what, twelve years old? One of those albums of movie stars came out, you know the kind where as you bought the candies you matched up the pictures on the wrappers and pasted them in. Real photographs, I don't know how they did it. Actresses like Betty Grable barelegged, on tiptoes in a boat. Betty Hutton in shorts sitting with her legs crossed, leaning back on her hands. And there was that girl Barbara Payton, Effol Flynn's mistress, who had terrific cleavage. Lana Turner in a bathing suit. And Tarzan's first Jane, practically nude.

—But they were all sort of innocent, you know? I remember one picture from an American movie that had something really sexy about it, it was Jane Russell, on top of a haystack, teasing Billy the Kid.

—You know who I worshiped was Rita Hayworth. Ah, *Salome* in that transparent dress made out of veils or something, she was half reclining on a—what did they call it—a *canape*, remember?

—Hot, really hot. And what about Gilda? That black satin strapless—"hope-it-falls" we called it—with a slit down the front.

—I remember a picture of her that came out in *Screen Scene*. She was stretched out, one leg extended and the other crossed over, her bust turned toward the camera, you could see the shape of her hips, bare legs, delectable!

—*Screen Scene*! That's where we first saw all the French film stars. It was X-rated.

—The Italian ones too. Remember Silvana Mangano picking rice in *Bitter Rice?*

—The first time I managed to see tits in the movies was when I was sixteen, seventeen years old.

—That was an incredible picture, incredible.

—I remember I got in with a fake ID. Nowadays even movies for ten-year-olds have naked women.

—Boy, did I make a mess of that picture, had to tear out the page and hide it.

—What was the name of that blonde, the French one, the first pair of tits I saw in the movies? Shit, what the hell was her name?

—Brigitte.

—Brigitte, my ass. This was way before Brigitte. That little blonde, the one who played Caroline.

—Martine Carol.

—Martine Carol! Right! The first tits I saw, unharnessed in the wind. I was already going to the Zone and everything but I wasn't old enough to see tits in the movies, imagine.

—Remember her famous bath scene, in *Lucretia Borgia*?

—It sounds like we were sex maniacs or something. That's what they'd call us nowadays, anyway. Degenerates.

—No kidding. But all I could think about was: girls' gym class, dirty magazines, movies, books, I saw sex in everything. Ha, it really does sound kind of degenerate!

—Macho boys were like that, had to be.

—And once you start remembering you can't stop. Did you see the picture with, what was her name, Rosana Podesta, with her wet blouse slicked to her chest? Holy shit.

—Memory is something else, boy. Amazing how those movies stayed with us. Sitting here talking about them I can see everything perfectly in my head. Like a photogram, just punch the button and the scene pops up.

—Françoise Arnoul, in nothing but panties, the camera zooming in close, practically licking her body. Scandalous for those days.

—And then those buxom Italians came on the scene.

—Silvana Pampanini. Remember that famous photo of her, holding her breasts like this? Not like she's hiding them, not at all, it was half-obscene, like she was weighing them or something. And then there was Gina Lollobrigida with that incredible cleavage, and Sophia Loren. She held her breasts like that, too, when she played Cleopatra. God knows I screwed them all.

—One day I was on my way out of the movies, some French film, when a guy called me aside out of the crowd and asked me in a half whisper, real anxious, is it dirty, huh? Is it?

—A young guy?

—No, a grown man.

—Right . . .

—Boy, the way we hoarded all that stuff, hidden away, as if we were actually jealous.

—I kept it all in that little closet under the stairs. Pictures, dirty books . . .

—Did you read *Anita's Presence?*

—Again and again. There was one part where Anita screws some young kid. We all used to imagine it was us. At least I did. Probably everybody did. I read his other book, *Dawn Without God.* And the things that would turn up at school, too, like the letter from the bride telling her friend all about the honeymoon, hand-typed stuff.

—Underground.

—Ha, ha. You got it!

—We used to make extra copies to sell.

—I read one called *Countess Gamiani.*

—*Memoirs of a Nun.*

—*Memoirs of a Singer.*

—*The Flophouse.*

—Ah, but that's the type you had to slog through to get to the dirty parts.

—You know there are some juicy passages in Jorge Amado, too.

—Uh-huh. I even found some pretty good stuff in *For Whom the Bell Tolls.*

—I'd say we were pretty degenerate.

—What about *Flesh?* How could I forget *Flesh!*

—Son-of-a-bitch, I read that book too many times, you know what I mean?

—"And a kiss sealed the scream forever in the throat of the virgin . . ."

—". . . who had just ceased . . ."

—". . . to be one."

—". . . to be one." That book was famous.

—And then years later, when we were grown up already, along came Brigitte Bijou, Henry Miller, the memoirs of Sir Henry Spencer Ashbee.

—The Fraud.

—Cassandra Rios, Sade, and lots more. Carlos Zefiro. The best . . . It was tough in those days to get hold of the really heavy-duty books. We ended up reading passages of books, the rest was usually so boring, we'd hunt and hunt for something sexy here and there, looking for pay dirt.

—That was hard work. Nowadays, books, movies—hell, real life! Kids have it a lot easier.

—Yeah, but the mystery is gone.

—Poof.

(The men nibble at the red tips of hot dogs, licking the oozing fat, they chew, they swallow. They feed themselves.)

—The days of intricate maneuvering to conquer a woman, the days of subtlety, are over. A lost art.

—It's true, you know how couples sit in bars these days, they're not even thinking about sex, just chat about this and that, distracted. It's not until it's time to leave that the guy says how about stopping at my place, or let's go to a motel. Just like that, no atmosphere.

—Or else it's the girl who does the suggesting.

—Really. And they're the same way. Casual. If you don't go through all the buildup, how can screwing be that ultimate sensational moment?

—They don't know how to concentrate.

—That's what it is, a lack of concentration. A lack of closeness.

—There's no suspense, no creativity.

—Right.

—No metaphor.

—No what?

—Metaphor, imagination, dreaming, nurturing, style.

—Right. No secrecy, either. No sin.

—None of that business of taking charge of the situation, where the man decides when, where, how . . . where he makes it last a little longer, takes a break, then starts up again.

—No evocation. Where all your past fucks come back to you in a flash.

—No sense of security. Women are so, so . . . indecent. So expert, so sure of themselves.

—So hungry. So demanding.

—You know what it is, there's no peace and quiet anymore, you know, just that wonderful darkness, your eyes closed, nothing else.

—No one to mess things up. No one.

—Just the dream, the voyage.

—The solitude.

)

Here we have the celebrated skirt-chaser waiting for his ballerina at the door to the den of vice. Fatigue, a slight case of gas, and a touch of nausea would never induce this gallant to keep a lady waiting, much less deprive his muff-tickler of something to tickle. So here we have him, furtive in his auto, watching the couples trickle out of the bar, waiting for his captivating concubine to emerge from the door. He looks at his watch and, how can this be, it's two-thirty: he must have fallen asleep. He walks up to the door with a hesitant step—shame on you, Sir Henry—and, incredulous, listens as the doorman tells him that Elisabete didn't come to work tonight, Bete called in sick. A gentleman like Sir Henry would under normal circumstances reply: "Are you absolutely certain?" rephrasing his question and asking for some further explanation; but, taken by surprise, the fine and elegant Sir Henry Spencer Ashbee burst out with a disastrous: "So you're covering for the slut, is that it, you faggot?" and it was Sir Henry's misfortune that the one thing this particular door-man could not tolerate being called was a faggot. So here we have the indomitable libertine flat-out on the sidewalk, quite an extraordinary predicament really, without fully understanding what happened. He struggles to his feet, realizing that it's time to retire to his mansion, let out the greyhounds, and redouble the guard. The worst of it is that now he's stone cold sober, the taste of blood lingering in his mouth, in a truly dismal mood. Driving home, he searches with his tongue for the cut inside his cheek. He approaches the house bobbing like a prize fighter, left guard up, right fist coiled like a spring; the spring releases a jab in the dark, one-two, he ducks, one-two, he ducks again, see the champion dance, observe his feet, how they fly, a quick right and he's alone in the ring, stand up and fight you clown, protector of whores.

Here we have Mr. de Moura, father of three—an eighteen-year-old son and two daughters, fifteen and sixteen—in front of the mirror, perplexed. He closes his eyes, shutting out the image, rinses his mouth with tepid water, runs his tongue over the cut, it's nothing, verifying that there are no external marks, turns off the light and goes into the bedroom, where he finds a note: mother called. "The old bag," he murmurs, puts on his pajamas and: bed.

And now here's the insomniac, the modem man, the victim, running through tomorrow at the plant, caressing a leg from yesterday, a dark pubis, that damned strike, thinking, well, at least some good has come from it, as far as uniting the management. Everyone was always trying to fuck the next guy and now here he was emerging the natural leader, accepted, our chalice in your hands now. Observe the victim, the saviour, sacrificing himself for the good of the company at three-something in the morning, worrying about the report that has to be letter-perfect. He telephones Elza and her voice is different from the daily "Yes, Mr. De Moura," "Fine, Mr. de Moura," as she explains that everything was going fine but she had to stop because she doesn't have the wage index set by the government in '73, she called him earlier to try to get the information. And no one left me a message? thinks the master of the house, pissed off, and here we have the perfect executive exerting his memory and coming up with the exact figure, with background music, Frank Sinatra, drifting into the room via the telephone, and he asks if she's been held up for long, and she says yes—"but I just took a little break"—and her voice does sound different, maybe because she's tired, maybe it's the voice of a woman in nightclothes. How can you work with that music, he wants (wants?) to know, aren't you likely to mix up the figures? and she must have noticed the difference in his voice by now, intimate like hers, or was she the one who was imitating his tone? but no, she only put the music on after she stopped working, that's all, waiting for his call. Mmmmm, the simple fact of a woman sitting waiting for his phone call at three A.M., ah, life. Would you like me to come over and give you a hand? suggests Sir Henry Spencer Ashbee stroking his muff-monger, Elza perhaps just in her panties in the hot night saying no, no, not now, and Sir Henry suddenly understands, it's crystal clear now, the failures of the day were all leading up to this, to the sensual smile on the other end of the telephone, to those freckles which spill down from her shoulders like ants, delicate specks on the skin above her breasts, never quite reaching them, saving them, tamed, for the great satyr now approaching with his swollen two-by-eight, inflamed with desire—"just give me the address, I'll be right over"—but now she's alarmed, no, really, no, please, my boyfriend's here, he's asleep. Ough, says the inveterate fucker, disappointed, British, before bidding a cordial good night to Miss Elza, already the family man lamenting the loose ways of young girls today.

And here he is, finally; here we have Omar Pires de Moura in his fever, his rapture, his sweet rendezvous: quest, voyage, dream, flight, approach, landing. Here we have him, forlorn, fumbling in the dark of night for Maria Eugênia, for her smooth thighs in the girls' gym class, thighs so close to him at fourteen and yet untouchable, always, baggy dark blue shorts showing them off more than protecting them, those smooth, sunburned, prohibited thighs, standing out from all others; here we have him shrinking back from the impossible possibilities of that proferred smile, "I love you" in his notebook in her handwriting, like an invitation to the little niche under the stairs, come to me, come to me; and here comes the hand of fear to calm his ardor, groping for past present past present past present past; here we have the two of them side by side in the cable car, her blue pleated skirt hiding the lustrous thighs which search for him with a secret, almost suffocating pressure, and before he knows it, it's happened, the first time ever without twiddling his turkey-neck, and with her there beside him feeling him throb and quake along with the cable car's irregular jerking, *nhem-nhem, NHEM, nhem*—everyone on the field trip must know by now, he's got to hide the stain with his school bag! Here we have him running away, twined around Luz del Fuego like a snake, a brute, bipartite beast, simultaneously penetrating and embracing, going into the carnival ball at Rio's Municipal Theater with Luz del Fuego, strolling out again with Luz del Fuego in the magazine *O Cruzeiro*, impressive and slightly shocking, exhausting himself, exhausting her in that two-headed embrace, going in, in, in while Rita Hayworth slowly removes her long, black satin gloves, skintight and sinuous, Aphrodite rising from the black satin strapless gown, already-bare arms, shoulders, the swells of her breasts, *amado mio, love me forever,* her thighs peeking from the slit down the front of the dress, and here we have him inserting his two-by-eight while Gilda, the Cytherian, responding to his touch, sucks in her stomach, a paroxysm of desire beneath the black satin, sensing his blind search for the exact spot, a shivering Aphrodite, an alabaster column just now emerging from a sea of satin; first one breast blooms, then the other, free at last, free of the code, the decency, pure beauty denied to the millions but revealed to him in secret thousands of times, a goddess born of light, receiving him, enclosing him, absorbing him, absorbing his excess, his fever, his rapture, his sweet rendezvous, while her brilliant teeth, a hallucination, nibble away at her Brazilian lover, the international playboy who's screwed nine out of ten movie stars, taming Gilda herself with his rod of steel—Gilda whom even Glenn Ford hadn't managed to break—and Jane Russell, too, learned her lesson on that haystack in the barn, so utterly alluring with a piece of hay between her teeth, coming on to Omar the Kid without wanting to put out, it's an old trick, they all do it, nostrils flaring open and closed like butterfly wings, desperate not to miss one whiff of that macho smell, her chest heaving in rhythm, filled to bursting with those aromas, nourishing blood and brain with the musky energy and excitement of

the hard-on she provoked, breasts swelling until they no longer fit inside
her blouse, but here's the Kid to liberate them, delight in them, offering
a sucked orange to someone who's thirsty, ha, ha, ha, tender pouches of
liquid, erect nipples as stoppers, or, when he's on top, swells descending
toward his open mouth like two bunches of grapes, he could cup them in
his hands like Silvana Pampanini in that photo, a puzzle: how many kilos
do I hold in these hands with red fingernails, her lips and eyes posing the
question: and how many kilos would *you* like, sir? offering them up to him,
always distant, the bitches, always unattainable and formidable, sophis-
ticated Iaras, offering themselves like Rosana Podesta emerging from the
sea in a wet, see-through blouse, two trembling, salty fish captive in the
fine net of fabric, and the footprints she leaves behind in the sand: tracks
to assist her pursuer; but first to appear in this scene are those siren breasts,
and he sneaks up behind her, crouched over, his hands cupped and ready,
sliding over the velvety sand, and in one lunge he has them in the palms
of his hands, pressing against her from behind, holding her firmly as she
struggles, arms and elbows tightly around her hips, preventing her from
turning or fleeing, enclosing her between his hips and his furious member;
but somehow she frees herself and: now you're going to get it, this will
teach you to lead me on like that, tum, tum, tum, and she falls submissive
on the sand, her two fish free of their net, flashing their salt spray in the
sun, and she presents them to him on the appetizing tray of her torso,
no longer fleeing but submissive, greedy, opening up for him, ravenous,
guiding his kingfisher as it dives and emerges, comes and goes, past
and present, past present past present past present past present, his
flight, his voyage, his sweet rendezvous with Maria Montez, possessed
a thousand and one nights, a veil calling attention to the tamarind
mouth, the seven veils which can't mask the beautiful dunes of her ass,
breasts loose beneath red silk, swaying like odalisques on an Arabian
horse galloping through the desert, a falcon on their trail; the flight,
the dive, the attack, the fall, the threatening crescent of glinting steel,
the cave of buried treasure finally unveiled, moan after moan under a

waning moon, the softness of Scheherazade recovered once and forever, possessed, a thousand and one nights: his dream, his approach,
his landing, his—ah—pleasure.

Here we have him, composed once more, the expert executive,
the genius with figures, seated at the long table in the factory cafeteria
at nine A.M., smiling complacently as he listens to the arguments of
the workers, flashing his teeth: proof he's not scared they'd like to
knock them out, producing a pack of cigarettes and offering them
around democratically, what a nice guy, look at this, lighting his
pals' cigarettes—that's what he calls them, "cigarette, pal?"—with his
butane lighter, such a charming fellow just now getting acquainted
with these dark folk from the land of Vera Cruz, a magic moment;
meanwhile the shaman's counterclaim in response to the proposed
wage agreement almost ruins the spell cast by the democratic Euro-
pean lighter lighting the democratic *Vera Cruz* cigarettes. The lighter
passes from hand to hand, click after magical click, fascinating one
and all with its slippery steel, polished to the point of—but, wait—he's
offering the magic fire to the last man, the dark one on his left, with
a sporting "It's yours, keep it," which has good repercussions on the
whole dark group, nodding approval, distracted from the words of
their shaman. Listen now as he responds, explaining with delicacy
and an abundance of excuses that the shaman's statistics are naïve,
that the country's economy is not based on beans, rice, and rent, and
he invites a committee of the strikers to his office to study together all
the particulars, to come to understand what stabilizes the government
which is, after all, "everybody's boss"—what an expression, what a
find! It makes him almost a partner in troubles, worthy of their trust
(he believes), a man who understands law and order. Observe him as
he guides the dark-skinned men through the corridors of power, now
there they are, sitting nervously on the edge of the sofa in the office of
the fabulous executive, without the courage to mention that the coffee is a trifle bitter, drinking with smiles all around so as not to offend

him, attentively listening to his explanations, their eyes following the
well-manicured finger as it traces curves on the chart, thin red, blue,
yellow, and black lines which signify that the maximum pay raise can
only be fifteen percent. There, in that nave from which he directs
the finances of the company, the wise executive presents his guests
with the report and accompanying chart, a mirror reflecting the entire
situation. Meeting over, mission complete, well done, in spite of the
concessions he had to make the efficient executive summoned Elza-
the-suave in order to dictate a letter to the president, and realized only
then that she was acting a little skittish, maybe because of his phone
call last night, a letter which would inform the president of the new
strategy—direct contact—he'd discovered for negotiating with the
workers, and of the excellent reception they gave the proposal, which
will make for excellent relations with the corporation, and he also
realized that Elza's delicate little breasts were rising and falling, breathless, in the rhythm of his dictation, thus it can be inferred from this
first meeting with the workers that, cognizant of the positive impact
it will have on their salaries, they will contribute in good faith toward
a raise in production, which will surely benefit the firm, and he still
couldn't help staring at how her nipples discreetly announced their
excitation from inside the light blouse, especially in that they have accepted for now the reasonable and limited wage hike of fifteen percent,
assuming that what their leaders have already termed an acceptable
proposal will be ratified in the union meeting this afternoon, as Sir
Henry's hand advanced trembling, and so thanks to this new level
of understanding we may conclude that having sown good seed, and
taking care to water well in future, reaching for her breast, squeezing
the nipple between thumb and index finger so that it gave off a little
whimper of surprise and surrender, that is to say, if we treat these
people well, our actions will surely bear good fruit, and all our plans
shall be consummated.

FRIDAY NIGHT/ SATURDAY MORNING

"*and the day shalle come when whyte men corrupted by simylar eviles will take pleasure in shootyng theyr muskets and rifles as in a great hunte.*"

(Estevam de Saa Perdigão—Commemorative of the Discoverie of Lost Golde.)

JULINHO

He jumped into the ocean and drowned his sorrows. Then he came back onto the beach, trailing water, and sat down beside her as though it made no difference at all.

With his sea-salty gaze he seasoned the white flesh just under her armpit—the beginning of a breast yet not quite the breast—and following the line of her bikini top, began to section the tender skin, preparing a delicate beefsteak which he offered to his neighbor down the beach in the conch of his hand; the nipple: an olive. He carved the other breast with the same precise gestures of a maître-d', and already there were hands stretched out and waiting. At first no one seemed terribly interested in the slight curve of her belly, apparently waiting for choicer portions, but as the blade crested that most subtle of rises and began its most subtle descent, the hands pressed in closer, begging. The golden carpet under the triangle of her bikini he gave to no one: this he removed whole and sat enjoying its saltiness while she turned over to allow him to work on the back part. First, a large circular chunk which he offered

35

to a couple—plenty for two—and then that smaller part, further down and secret, which the man in the dark glasses was asking for.

—Christ, Julinho, what is it with you? You picked a great time to space out.

An hors d'oeuvre of tongue, the olives of her eyes, so he won't have to listen, or speak. Then a long incision in the inner thighs, an area disputed by everyone, but it just wasn't working: she had broken the spell.

—Okay.

—"Okay"? High as a fucking kite, that's what you are. Just look at your eyes.

—Lay off, will you?

—That's why it's just no good, Julinho, can't you see?

He turned her over to Zé Carlos, saying: She's all yours. Zé Carlos basted her with butter and Heitor and Hélio and Zé Carlos started fighting about who should get to screw her. The minute one of them got close, the other two began pushing and shoving and she slipped through their hands like a fish; even when their cocks slipped inside they slid right out again, all buttery. There was simply no way to tighten the knot of their embrace because the more she struggled the greasier she got, they were spending more time slip-sliding around than getting anywhere in particular, until one gets her in a fireman's carry, another holds her open, and the third goes inside: strength in unity. She mumbled something.

—Baby, I couldn't care less.

—Okay, *okay*. Let's just enjoy the beach, okay?

A boat crossing the bay. The man seated in the stern waits for the pretty blue marlin to go for the bait, his eyes shaded by a hat with a Ray-Ban visor. The fish sparkles like a silver globe in a nightclub ceiling, and its sword stabs at the bait which is yelling, Help, Julinho, help! but meanwhile the fisherman, annoyed, begins complaining about all the noise, you'll scare off the fish! He plays out the line so the bait sinks to the bottom, fish and bait both disappear; for a long while there's just the wide arc of water the boat draws behind, then all at once the bait pops to the surface.

—Shit, Julinho, I mean I can't deal with you when you're like this. Shit, Julinho.

He looked at her and how should he know, after all, why she was crying? Back to the fishing.

DEODATO

A Deus Dat = Given to God.

Destiny: Southern Cross/Southern Cruzeiro$.

Work card, dead tired, work work:

Whitewash of Summer.

Brick of Fall.

Steel of Winter.

Paint of Spring.

Cement of Harmony.

And: prick, useless pendant, thick. (The women leave you hanging.)

Life: a hard-fought battle in which the weaklings are overcome: don't cry, son.

—In my country there are palm trees.

And: this feeling of missing: what could it be for?

As to health, with whose wealth? The sauba ant eats health, lungs, cruzeiros, work, desire, the South, but not the palm trees: unforgettable.

The short missile, missive, epistle: "Rained up there yet? Nothin' but dreams down here, mama, dad. Tell the guy who brings this if it rained yet 'cause if it rained I'm on my way home. Bless me, father, mother. Deodato."

The wait: hospital, etc., etc.

The discharge: back to the hovel, the hole.

The wait on the hard floor. Beating off and beat.

Message received, message returned: Yes, it rained it's all green and growing. Bless you son bring a radio so we can listen to the radio.

Wait turned to hope.

Counting the days: the day of accounting.

Accounts settled: one talisman, one stabbing, one takeoff.

Ready set go destiny: God-given North.

DANIVAL

Danival does what he can. What he can't do he hides when he does. What he doesn't do hasn't been done. What he hasn't done isn't done. When he can't, he leaves it for later. The only reason he wouldn't is if he wasn't allowed, but he's allowed. And another thing: he doesn't do what they tell him to. If they tell him to, he doesn't. He only does things with no schedule and no instructions. He only does what he does and he only did it when he wanted to. And he likes what he's doing while he's doing it; but as for doing things because he has to, forget it.

Danival is, was, would be.

And did, does, would do: hand out slips of paper advertising plumbers and fortune-tellers; sell peanuts at soccer games; sell kites at beaches and parks; sell lottery tickets from behind a table on Avenue Atlántica; wash cars; rent out cardboard for people to tape on their windshields while they're at the beach so the sun won't heat up the seats; sell little jars of soap bubbles; sell cotton candy at fairs; carry baskets for people at outdoor markets; scalp tickets at big soccer games; guard cars during samba rehearsals; hand out slips of paper endorsing candidates for political office; buy and sell old newspapers, magazines, empty bottles, broken gadgets; shine shoes; hawk special editions of the newspaper; hunt through the trash for anything useful; deal pot; fix roofs after hailstorms; sell porno magazines; sell ice-cream out of a Styrofoam cooler at sporting events; collect bets for numbers-runners; put posters up around town; help erect circus tents; fish for mussels and crab; sell slides of naked women set in little plastic viewers to the peons on big construction sites on payday, etc.

And one day Danival meets Maria do Carmo, Carmo, Carminha.

And so changed the tense of the verb, the present being passed at her side.

And it was then that the best happenings happened.

She had a plan: bungalow, television, table with tablecloth, two chairs (eventually four), bed complete with sheets and blankets, gas range. It could happen in stages, everything in its time, but she had to have them all: "That's the way I was brought up." She contributed the little she'd made in the life on Highway Dutra. And gave up the life.

She gave herself to him.

And that was when Danival became an automobile mechanic in a garage on Highway Dutra, near Nova Iguaçu.

And it was mainly then that the unreliable, incapable, transient Danival, that shifty, troublesome, uncontrollable, drunken, unpredictable, braggart Danival, incorrigible, free-spirited, curious, vagrant, clever, dangerous, tamed, irritable, shameless and resigned Creole changed his loose, short, and useless life.

He gave himself to her.

And remains given.

Said and done.

ZÉ CARLOS

—Buy me a sandwich, ma'am?

And she did. Out of pity—the night was warm and happy—she ordered an extra hamburger from the guy behind the counter and stared at the girl: filthy dirty, thirteen maybe, with grimy white skin, and a tear in the right side of her dress which exposed one small breast almost entirely.

—You should find yourself something better to wear, dear. At your age! You can't go around like that anymore, just look at you.

The girl said nothing, she was looking toward the lunch counter, and had clasped her right arm over the tear, which ran all the way from her shoulder to the curve of her ribs.

—Your mother lets you go out like that?

The girl said yes, yes, she does, looking emphatically toward the young man who held a plate with a hamburger on it, then at the hamburger itself as it passed from his hands to the woman's to her own; then she mumbled God bless you and disappeared somewhere to eat. The woman lectured the young lady with her—daughter? niece?—on the subject of parental neglect and the horror of poverty, just think, at this hour a young girl her age should be doing her homework, she was just filthy, did you see? It's obvious she never bathes, poor thing, I'll bet they don't even have running water, it's absurd, whatever happened to the idea of governmental responsibility, how many more like her are there in Brazil, she said as she ate, that girl is taking some risk, out in the streets like that at night, with little breasts already—pretty ones, even—she can't just walk around the streets half-naked, and then the girl was back, over near the lunch counter talking to two guys. The woman pretended to throw something in the trash so she could get close enough to overhear the tail end of their conversation.

The girl: Sure, okay.

One guy to the other: Wait here, Julinho. Ten minutes.

He crossed the street, walked down the sidewalk, and disappeared onto the beach. The woman went on talking with her daughter or niece, they got in line for ice-cream, the girl too had disappeared; they ate their ice-cream, the daughter or niece insisted on another, even if it would make her sick, all that ice-cream at this hour, so they got in line again, the crowd was thinning, and were just about ready to leave when the woman noticed the girl making her way back from the beach toward the restaurant. Then the boy appeared, crossed Avenue Atlántica, strolled in and paid for two ice-cream cones, handing the receipt to the girl, who went to pick them up at the counter. All at once the woman understood, distressed, and called her over:

—Honey! Come here for a minute.

The guy who had paid for the ice-cream made as if to leave, hands in his pockets, not the least bit concerned.

—What did that fellow do to you?

The young lady beside her, scandalized: Auntie, don't! but the woman didn't give her time to finish, glared at him, sputtering:

—You shameless lout!

Everyone staring by now, the niece dying of embarrassment.

—Degenerate! But, honey, for an ice-cream cone! Why didn't you say something? I would have bought you one. Call the police, somebody, that degenerate abused this girl, he was wearing a red silk shirt and light-colored pants—quick, he went that way, he can't have gone far.

He was invisible. No one moved, the niece knowing it was a pointless outcry, the woman still cajoling:

—What did he do to you, honey?

The girl, without saying a word, just licked the tip of her ice-cream, and smiled.

MIGUEL

He was doing everything right, keeping his distance, keeping his guard up, getting in a good jab now and then at his opponent, suddenly delivering a rapid combination, then going back to the jab, feeling totally confident, which is why he doesn't know how he ended up here, down on his knees with that loud ringing in his ear, the world wobbling back and forth, the referee standing over him counting:

One

Shouts, whistles, that wobbling sensation. He shakes his head and re-members: a left cross to his ear and the world disappeared for a second, then came back, then wouldn't stop wobbling, this couldn't be happening.

Two

Might as well take advantage of each second and rest a little. He'd rest six seconds; when the referee gets to nine he'll get up, because he can't lose this fight—why was it he couldn't lose this fight?

Three

A nice little rest. His brother knows what's happening, knows he's waiting for the right moment to get up, it's a well-known trick in boxing, everybody knows that, but Juverci doesn't know that.

Four

No reason to hurry just because of that, lose a few seconds' rest just because she's here. The worst thing to do would be to get up before he's ready, might even lose him the fight. Falling down's no disgrace, the disgrace is not getting up.

Five

Juverci doesn't know what's going on because she never wanted to know anything about boxing, she says it's no way to make a living, but what about Éder Jofre—all the money he made? So he asked her to come to the fight, insisted really, so she'd see how good he was, and was he good.

Six

He made a deal with her: you come watch me fight and if you think I'm no good I'll give it up. That's why—to show her that's why he was going to leap up like an animal and finish off that bastard. Right there: the bastard's left was way down.

Seven

That's exactly where he was going to land his right, a real bomb. That puny jerk, bobbing around the ring like a monkey. He could hear the feet bouncing, bouncing, and Juverci not understanding what the hell was going on. You wait, you little faggot, you just wait.

Eight

When the referee says nine he's going to get up, fast. Then the referee will give the word, the faggot will come at him with his left low and he'll slide a right straight to the chin. One punch is all he needs. He was just resting.

Nine

Now! He wants Juju to see exactly what he's going to do, gonna end that fight with one good punch. Juju must be miserable with him there on the floor. She didn't understand what was happening, that he was just resting a little.

Ten

Just resting a little.

HEITOR

(   )

"But I'm at the end of my rope, Heitor. I wrote you a letter just yesterday, explaining the situation—you'll understand when you get the letter."

(   )

"Everything. Things you just can't explain on the telephone. I'm pretty desperate here, Heitor, I don't know what I'm going to do.

(   )

"I did, really I did, I tried everything, Heitor. And it *is* the real thing: I've been nauseous for a week now, all the time, frantic because I wasn't able to talk to you. That's why I wrote that letter yesterday, I didn't know how else to get in touch with you. What am I supposed to do, Heitor?

(

)

"I know very well I'm not a child, you don't have to be rude."

(   )

"Of course that's what you meant. I know *that* much about you."

(
)

"I already did. There's no one around here, Heitor. I was so upset the other day I even talked to a friend of mine, but she didn't know anything either, she said there isn't anyone here in Campos, at least not that she ever heard of."

(   )

"Who? Are you crazy? Do you think I go around with people like that, *here,* people who are into things like that? You don't know my family, Heitor, you don't understand the situation. This is a very delicate thing, I don't know why you can't see that."

(
)

"That won't help either, I want to get this taken care of as soon as possible."

(   )

"The longer this drags on, the harder it is for me, Heitor. I have to get this taken care of right away. I've been trying to get in touch with you for two weeks now, I couldn't reach you at work, they told me you'd gone out, you were coming back later, you hadn't arrived yet. I'm sorry for calling you at home."

(   )

"Uh-huh, they gave it to me."

(   )

"A woman."

(   )

"What else could I do, Heitor? I couldn't get you at work, I even thought, well, maybe you didn't want to talk to me."

(
)

"But I wanted to let you know I'll be coming next week."

(   )

"What? You can't do this to me, Heitor . . ."

( )

"Oh no you're not. You'll just have to put off your trip. You've got to be there. And you're going to find a doctor and make an appointment for me. It's the least you can do, Heitor."

(
)

"I know, I know. I'm sorry. But who else can I turn to? I've been beside myself over all this, and then the nausea . . . I know it's tough for you, too, but you're a man, Heitor. And I've got to hide this from everyone, even from that friend of mine, and we go way back."

( )

"I told her it was for somebody else, naturally she'd never think it was for me. No one here would think that."

( )

"Of course. I know. The problem is I can't wait, that's all."

(
)

"Of course I wouldn't assume something like that. Don't worry, I'll pay. I just want to get this over with."

(
)

"Okay, fine. You set up the appointment and call me. No, maybe it's better if you don't call. I'll be there on Monday. What?"

( )

"Right, don't worry. I'll bring a little extra. See you Monday."

ADILSON

The ceremony began Saturday morning: he took out two hundred fifty cruzeiros to buy his first pair of pajamas, a purchase he'd been planning for three months, ever since he got a job collecting bus fare, though until that Saturday he hadn't been able to buy them because so much was needed at home, his father was out of work; two of his younger brothers, twelve and eleven, made a little money rounding up old newspapers in better neighborhoods—also scrap metal, empty bottles, and household junk, which sometimes people gave them for free when the stuff was just taking up space, but the little they made was barely enough for the daily milk and meat, there was never anything left; his other two brothers, eight and six, didn't work, except for helping out at home—sweeping, dusting the furniture, running down to the corner market for things, so the money just didn't stretch far enough to allow him the luxury of buying a pair of pajamas; and they wouldn't even have had money for the essentials—food, rent, car fare, notebooks for school—if he hadn't been lucky enough to appear at the bus company the same day they fired a kid, the bus driver had refused to work with him anymore, he kept getting into fights with passengers over change, and the manager had looked over his papers and warned him: Make any trouble and you're back on the streets, there's no shortage of people looking for work, you know; those were his only instructions besides filling him in on company policy: at the end of the day when it was time to settle accounts, if he came up short it would be taken out of his salary, the boss didn't want to hear about it; on the other hand, anything extra was his, no need even to mention it; this was obviously a good system and he accepted the job immediately, first because he had always been good at math, second because he already had experience making change from when he worked for Mr. Pepepê at the outdoor market—Mr. Pepepê had a bad stutter and needed someone to speak up quickly when people asked the price of a particular vegetable or to bargain with customers—and third because he had to, they were practically going hungry at home, and no one wanted to give his father a job because of his age; it was hard even for *him* to get a job, because he was almost eighteen and would have to go into the service soon; no one wanted to train him at something and lose him to the Army in less than a year, better to hire a fourteen-year-old; that's why, for the past three months there had never been any money left over, until his father gave up looking for a regular job and started doing odd jobs—plumbing repair, painting, brick-laying, anything and everything he knew how to do, going from house to house and building to building in the fancy neighborhoods, and he'd been doing pretty well lately, well enough for his oldest son to set aside two hundred fifty cruzeiros from his own salary to walk confidently into the Ducal in Nova Iguaçu one Saturday morning, ask to see a pair of pajamas, waver between the ones for a hundred and eighty and the ones for two hundred fifteen, buy the more expensive pair, and get on the bus for home satisfied with life, somewhat thrilled in anticipation of the enjoyment to come, and it was with these tender emotions in his heart that he dropped his package at home and went looking for his friend Miguel to have a beer before lunch and tell him about his purchase, describing in detail the style and color and shape of the pockets; that night he put on his pajamas and, even though it was Saturday, didn't go out: instead he watched TV and went to bed early; Sunday morning, instead of putting on his blue jeans as usual and going for a stroll around the neighorhood, shirtless, showing off his bare torso as usual, he remained in his pajamas and sat out in front of the house, a house which sat on a precipice and had no garden wall around it and no gate either, because his father believed "poor people don't need to be afraid of robbers"; and since the house was in the middle of the block, anyone walking up or down the street had to pass his striped pajamas, staring, admiring, and he cheerfully greeted everyone who walked by; he was the second or third person on the street to own a pair of pajamas, imagine, on the whole street, a dirt lane with sewer water rushing through the ditches on either side, which made for problems with ball control playing soccer, and also made for lots of mosquitoes at night; but the high point of that Sunday of pleasures was going to the bar, about three blocks below the house, to pick up a couple of beers for lunch, dressed in his blue jeans and pajama top, stared at all the way, and on his way back the *buzz-buzz*ing of a group of girls standing at the gate, and out of the *buzz-buzz*ing hearing something or other quite clearly about his extraordinary blue-striped pajamas.

HÉLIO

If someday we get caught, which of us would be able to say how it all started, why, whose idea it was, how it became the Friday night agenda, who was the organizer, who chose time, place, victims: who could explain how this thing moved from fiction to reality? Who knows the whole story? Not one of us.

Someone should have been taking notes—about our thoughts, even the trivial ones, our gestures, our notions of the world: maybe all those things would be necessary to understand? During the week, I myself see these Friday night/Saturday mornings from a distance, in a vague sort of way: someone else's actions: images: a film out of sequence. The same way I see myself as a boy: another person, a film, isolated scenes. We are all creatures born of the coupling of fear and happiness, products with no guarantee—or, if not, then how is it that this "other" can begin to be born in us, this other who is capable of things we were not?

And, when? During childhood? First, there is born inside us, inside each boy, a boy who is not afraid of the dark. No more subtle noises, figures, signs of some trap being laid for us in the invisible blackness—and so the dark becomes a hiding place, a way of escaping the kick in the pants or the spoonful of medicine. Or is he born in us the moment father is no longer the miracle man and mother is not just the woman who changes our clothes, feeds us, bathes us, and watches over our sleep? Born in us with our parents' changing roles: the authority figure and the mater-martyr? They begin to give us tasks, puzzles, they buy us pencils, erasers. Living is no longer just a matter of inventing, suddenly it means obeying; our time is no longer our own, we must ask to use it. In the boy of letters was there lurking already the man of numbers? The big citizen who kills the little citizen? Me, this businessman, married, three children, pissed at life—pissed at what, after all?—was he lurking somewhere there in the boy Mama called her little charmer?—poor Mama. Was the seducer of defenseless females already present in the furtive masturbator of the junior high? The TV voyeur in the boy-wonder of whores? And the righteous legislator of Friday evenings in the child exhibitionist, hero of schoolgirls?

Each of us has his motives of course. What's amazing and frightening is thinking of the hands that weave the web which brings these motives together and forms a group, various groups, plotting a national situation in which it's possible for us to act safely, confidently, the public divided between indifference, acceptance, and solidarity. Has this all been orchestrated somehow? How could we have discovered the chance, the moment to jump in, if not for some maestro's hand waving us on: trumpets! enter trumpets! My God, for someone to talk to about the solemnity and the mystery, instead of just three idiots who don't even understand the difference between them and the police squads, who have absolutely no conception of the subtle combination of circumstances which make a given action possible at a particular historical moment.

With what expectations do *they* prepare for tonight? Julinho's snorting coke, no doubt. Heitor's probably in some bar telling dirty jokes to the happy-hour crowd. Zé Carlos is out pinching ass somewhere, a degenerate prowling the schoolyard. I'm the only one waiting for the moment with the elegance, the confidence, and the intellectual anguish of a white hunter.

VALTINHO

Válter was born at seven months, of a black father and a more-or-less black mother, the fifth of seven children.

Sick off and on through most of his childhood, by and large looked after by his older siblings, he got very little attention from his mother who had to do other people's laundry.

Hardly knew his father, who was involved in the numbers racket and was killed by another racketeer.

Did poorly in elementary school in Queimados, studying only up to third grade.

Had mumps when he was nine, which untreated degenerated into an inflammation of the testicles, which explains the origin of the nickname Valtinho Balloon-Balls, a name which made him pale with rage.

Made himself a bow and arrow out of bamboo and wounded a boy named Beiçola one time, which earned him the nickname Valtinho Robin Hood, of which he approved.

Contracted—almost all at once—measles, chicken pox, whooping cough, and verminosis, and spent an extended period sick in bed, giving rise to yet another nickname by the time he was back on the streets: Valtinho Sickout, which is the one that stuck.

Sold roast peanuts at soccer games.

Worked as a "beach rat" for Zezinho Nice Guy, snatching money and belongings people left on the beach when they went swimming.

Had ambitions to work on his own but got beat up by Zezinho Nice Guy.

Was picked up during one of his swings down the beach, the crowd yelling, "Stop, thief!"

Was sent to Juvenile Court and from there to the reformatory, where he was initiated into the pain of anal sex.

Escaped six months later.

Was lookout at a drop-off point for pot deals on Two Brothers Hill.

Had sex for the first time at age twelve with a black girl as everyone held her down and each took turns screwing her in a dark corner of Curral das Éguas.

Picked pockets at outdoor markets.

Was picked up for vagrancy (sleeping on a park bench), got a beating at the precinct, and was sent from there to Juvenile Court, then back to the reformatory.

Screwed a boy who liked to be screwed.

Escaped (with the boy) after three months.

Pickpocketed around town with Beiçola, Pastelzinho, and Quinzão.

Dealt pot on Two Brothers Hill, finally King of the Mountain.

Bought a gun and killed Zezinho Nice Guy.

Became friendly with Maria Dilsa, age thirteen, who was always stoned on marijuana.

Paraded with Beija-Flor Samba Club from Nilópolis.

Killed Beiçola for ratting on him.

Was arrested and sentenced to twenty-eight years.

Escaped from Ilha Grande three years later.

Reclaimed Maria Dilsa from Quinzão at gunpoint and gave her a good beating to win her back.

Began dealing coke on Tijuca Hill.

Was drinking beer in a bar in Belfort Roxo when four armed men burst in shouting, "Police!" and "Nobody move!" and knew right away those fuckers were no policemen.

DESTINY

—Police!

A ripple of fear through the bar.

—Nobody move!

Oh shit, Jesus, Mary, and Joseph. Everyone smells danger.

—All of you, up against the wall!

Hair standing on end, God help us, guts threatening to explode any minute.

—Up against the wall, move it!

Maniacs: the shortest one, muscular, his finger on the trigger, nervous, turning every so often to look toward the door; the young one, blond, pushing everyone in the bar up against the wall, danger flashing in his green, crazed eyes; the one in the red shirt chewing gum, legs planted firmly, wide open, gun pointed, ah shit, Jesus, Mary, and Joseph; and the one whose dark hair was going gray, who seemed to be in charge, that's right, sir, he was the one calling the shots from the doorway, he told the others what to do, gun stuck in his pants, hand on the trigger, his eye on everything.

—All right, let's see some ID, fast!

Seven in the bar, eight with the owner, twelve with the four, thirteen with the devil. The blond and the short muscular guy check IDs, the muscular guy excuses the woman with a shove and, ah, here we are, you can bet we got one right here.

—Where do you work, kid?

—I don't work no more, I quit 'cause I'm on my way to Paraíba.

—Here's one for you.

He throws the ID to the man with the gray hair, who grabs it out of the air almost without taking his eyes of the street. That's when the mulatto on the end makes a run for it, and I'm sure it was Valtinho Sickout, officer, I've known him since he was a kid, knew his mother, she lived around here somewhere, and the mulatto knocks down everything in his path, including the blond, leaves him with a handful of shirt, that's right, I saw it too, there was the shirt but no Valtinho in it, he was out the door, his dark skin already blending with the dark night, when the guy in the red shirt, aiming with two hands, legs spread wide, bang bang bang and look, the mulatto's on the ground, Jesus, Mary, and Joseph, and the one with the gray hair and the muscular guy, guns in hand, making sure nobody else moves, the mulatto outside on the ground moaning.

—Okay, let's see your papers, you pack of dogs.

—This one here, this black boy comes with us.

—I've got a job, mister, I got a clean slate.

—Who asked you, shithead?

—But I'm a mechanic, I can show you, it's just down the street.

—I said shut up, boy!

He put the kid's ID in his back pocket. The woman moved toward him, got another shove.

—Over there, piranha.

The blond—still holding the mulatto's shirt, hate in his eyes, hate for the mulatto, hate for us all, all seven, Jesus, Mary, and Joseph, the peril in those eyes—choosing victims:

—I say we take these two.

The muscular one:

—Ah, two young punks—and into the booze already, eh?

—No, it's just beer, we were just having a beer.

—Sure, sure, and on whose money, you little j.d.'s?

—No, sir. Really. I've got a job, I work on the bus, I collect fares.

—And what about you, punk, how old are you?

—Eighteen.

—Yeah, and what do you do?

—I just got called up for the service, so, well, that's why I don't really have a job right now, at the moment.

The gray-haired boss, from the door, nervous:

—What the fuck is all the talk? Let's get going.

—What about the two punks?

—They come too. Let's move it.

The muscular guy and the blond, kicking and shoving, separate out the ones they're taking with them, a repetition of scenes which are commonplace by now in the climate of violence which prevails in Baixada Fluminense and which we have denounced daily within these pages. The woman:

—Can't I talk to him, please just let me talk to him.

She points to the one with the gray hair. The muscular guy laughs, Jesus God, that knowing laugh.

—Sure. Why not?

The woman:

—Please, sir, officer, don't take my man, please, he's got a job, don't take my man.

—The hell!

He smashes the woman over the head with his gun, see, the muscular guy knew all along, and blood spurts all over her hand, her face, and she falls, right over there, sir, that's right, right near the bar, and there was blood coming from her forehead, blood running down her hand, it was brutal, you had to see it, you know, and then he yells to his men, like he was in a hurry, like he was afraid of someone coming:

—All right! Let's go, let's get out of here. And I'll give you folks a little warning: anyone puts the finger on us and we'll be back.

The four are dragged off by the four, kicking, shoving, guns ready. The men who had identified themselves as police completed the familiar scenario by retreating to two automobiles parked nearby, a white Impala and a red Volkswagen, according to information we received from our sources, and speeding off via a route unknown. Two are pushed into the backseat of the red Volkswagen, the other two thrown into the trunk of the white Impala, and no doubt it's the gray-haired guy saying:

—Toss that half-dead mulatto in the trunk too.

One more groan from inside and bam, it closes with a bang; the cars take off, peeling rubber—so fast, according to the witnesses we spoke to, that it was impossible to take down the license plate numbers, and also because it was extremely dark. The people left in the bar cross themselves before rushing to help the woman, still sprawled on the floor, moaning.

INVESTIGATIONS

The Assistant Chief of Police on duty in Belfort Roxo takes the complaint early in the morning, as soon as he wakes up, and guarantees the woman with the head wound, who has been waiting to see him since eleven P.M.: (1) there'll be an investigation and (2) no, we're not the ones who picked him up, I'm telling you. At ten o'clock the Chief arrives and so does the news that five bodies have been found on the Vila de Cava Road. The Chief starts getting his team together, and calls Pedrão-38 off into a corner. (You know anything about this? No sir, not a thing. Are you sure? Give it to me straight, Pedrão. No, nothing. Not a thing.) and then says out loud:

—All right. Right this way, ma'am. Have you put some Mercurochrome on that?

—Yeah, somebody already took care of it.

—Good people we got here, huh?

It was them, the men from the bar, lined up on the ground, tortured, obviously, shot full of holes. The woman screams, cries: Danival, Danival, my baby, ay, my Danival, fucking sons-of-bitches, baby, love, Danival, and meanwhile the chief tells his crew to call in the medical examiners and the press. He waits patiently, irritated, for the woman to calm down a bit.

—What was he into? Pot? Cocaine?

—He was a mechanic, I already told you he was a mechanic.

The chief looks at the dead man's hands: nails caked with grease.

—Right, and what did he do on the side?

—Nothing, really, why don't you go over there, go to the garage and ask if he wasn't a good worker, ask if he had any time to get in trouble.

—Come on, sweetheart, I know this hood.

—But, sir, you couldn't, he wasn't like that, really.

Danival was wearing a tee-shirt that had an open mouth on the front with an enormous tongue hanging out, a pair of beat-up blue chinos, size 41 shoes, had a bullet hole in the left cheek, and the owner of the garage assured the chief:

—He was a good worker all right, eight A.M. sharp till seven at night.

—Damn.

—Never missed a day. Didn't drink on the job or anything, either. It's a shame, a hell of a shame.

He'd been living with Maria do Carmo for over a year, they rented a house in Mesquita, had a bullet hole in the left leg, a modest little house, one bedroom, living room, bathroom out back, gas range, paid the rent on time, had a bullet hole in the abdomen, refrigerator, and Monday a letter came through from Riachuelo that, yes, all payments were up to date.

—Damn.

The medical examiners take pictures, first of the five bodies lined up in a row, just as they were found, then they flip over the first in line and discover that Danival had a bullet hole in the back of the neck, made a living doing odd jobs before he met Maria do Carmo, apparently dealt a little pot for "The Head" some three years back, had several hematomas on the side of the head, but had a clean slate with "The Head," too, no rumors he was out looking for this Danival kid, and "The Head" doesn't leave things till next week, never mind three years later, had a bullet hole in the liver area, Tuesday National Identification Service announced they had nothing on record against him, a bullet hole in the left lung, his neighbors had no complaints:

—A hard worker, not much of a drinker, no not really.

—Damn black dude.

The first newspaper reporter arrives and then a reporter from a radio station. The Chief says he's not talking until every last one of them gets there, he's not going to tell the whole story over and over. The photographer keeps clicking the row of corpses, working alongside the medical examiners. They turn the second body face up, a mulatto. Pedrão-38 recognizes him:

—That's Valtinho Sickout! Chief! Hey, Chief! This one here is Valtinho Sickout!

—What did I tell you: a drug war.

Valtinho had a bullet hole in the eye, jeans, no shirt, bullet hole in the left cheek, a pair of sneakers which had once been white, a gold chain with an amulet around his neck, dealt both grass and cocaine as well as committing assaults in Queimados, Nova Iguaçu, Belfort Roxo, Rio, Campo Grande, and environs, had a bullet hole in the left side of the neck, and the owner of the bar provided confirmation:

—It's definitely Valtinho, Chief, no doubt about it. I've known him since he was a kid, I knew his mother.

The Chief tells them to get rid of the spectators: no rubberneckers, just the press and the frantic relatives of people who didn't come home last night. Worried faces approach nervously and then, relieved, hang around expecting a scene, waiting to see what it would have been like if they were the parents. The only victim known to the police is Valtinho, previously arrested for murder, incarcerated at Ilha Grande, got twenty-eight years, had been an unruly and sickly child, father killed by a guy in the numbers racket, a bullet hole in the right groin, when he was a boy Valtinho's mother would send him to Paulo "Linguiça" 's market to get bread and mortadela and eggs and Valtinho told everyone he didn't have to pay, people said his mother really put out but she wasn't as bad as all that, a bullet hole in the right thigh, lived with a seventeen-year-old girl named Maria Dilsa.

—I'm telling you he was not a gangster or a drug dealer. Mr. Danival was a mechanic.

—But the Chief says it was a drug war.

—I told the Chief, too, I told him he was a mechanic. Why won't he believe me?

—That's the way it is, unless you can prove it.

—Please don't put in the newspaper he was a gangster, mister, because he wasn't.

Danival liked soap operas, comedy programs, had a bullet hole in the left leg, smoked unfiltered cigarettes, liked tripe with lima beans, was becoming a real good engine mechanic. The Chief gets a call over the radio: there's a couple at the station who heard the description of the victims on the radio and think one of them is their son Adilson. Adilson was seventeen and a half years old, sneakers, jeans, a bullet hole in the right shoulder, Caucasian, average height, hadn't shaved that day and was growing a scraggly mustache, a bullet hole next to the right ear, straight hair which was always falling over his right eye and obstructing his vision, a bullet hole in the sternum, a blue turtleneck, and invariably pissed into the ravine down the street before coming in at night because the toilet was out in the pitch-black backyard. The Chief tells them to send the couple over right away before the bodies are taken to the morgue. Then he gathers together the press—print, radio, TV—and gives his official opinion which is that these killings represent one more round in the drug war going on between gangs in Baixada Fluminense and Rio de Janeiro, and Maria do Carmo corrects him:

—Danival was no gangster, how many times do I have to tell you?

—Shut up, piranha, murmurs a detective behind her, with a nudge.

The Chief insists that the presence of known drug trafficker Valtinho Sickout is a definite sign that what we're dealing with here is a gangland-style slaying, although the other victims have not yet been identified. Danival, for example, had no police record, was apparently never involved in anything serious, knew the National Anthem from memory, in fact won quite a few bets on it from people he happened to meet who thought they knew it too, had a bullet hole in the stomach, was not a crook, though his "odd job" past is suspicious. The squad car arrives from the precinct with the couple to identify the body of Adilson, who had a bullet hole in the right lung, really liked his job collecting bus fare, only last week had bought himself a pair of blue-striped pajamas, just started going with a neighborhood girl named Eunice, and had a slightly lackadaisical way of pushing back the hair which was always falling over his right eye.

—God in heaven, it's him, it's Adilson, oh son, oh God—Inácio, it's Adilson, our Adilson, oh my God!

The boy's father kneels down excruciatingly slowly, as if in one of those slow-motion sequences, until his knees finally touch the ground next to his son's head, his dead son's head, a touching photo for the front page, the photographer promises his editor, and the father's head and upper body and hands keep lowering until his head rests between his own knees and the boy's cold right cheek, oh, son, such a good boy, and he had a date for Sunday with that girl Eunice, in front of the Pavilhão moviehouse in Nova Iguaçu, just the third date and he was getting daring, he asked her not to wear a bra and she laughed, the little flirt, not promising anything but not saying no, either, and the man is immobile, bent over, no sobbing, no expression at all, in the Saturday Rio sun, everyone's at the beach, as if there was no one left there by the side of the road, not even his wife screaming at his side, no police, no photographers, just that perfect son who helped put bread on the table while his father was out of work, who loved to tell stories about the things that happened each day on the Belfort Roxo-Terminal bus, who used to bring home one light beer and one dark beer to go with Sunday dinner, who had a bullet hole in the left thigh.

The Chief calls to the woman and asks for some information about her son; he prefers to talk to her because the man seems to have gone dumb, he doesn't like to disturb people when they're like that and this way the woman will have to stop making such a racket: lately he just didn't have much patience for all the noise the victims' relatives made, always the same story.

—I need a vacation, Pedrão.

His name was Adilson Pinheiro Lima, son of Neide Torres Pinheiro and Inácio Campista Lima, Caucasian, seventeen years of age, educated through junior high school, resident of the Magalhães Bastos section of Miriam Gardens, employed by the Belrio Bus Company, a bullet hole in the right buttock, such a good boy, hardly ever went out at night, when he did it was with his girlfriend or his friend Miguel, another kid from the neighborhood, about the same age, a friend of his since grade school who was training Monday, Wednesday, and Friday to be a boxer at the Academy of Strength and Vigor in Rio, and Adilson came home early every night because he had to be at work at five A.M., bullet hole through the heart, and no, impossible, he never hung around with the wrong crowd or had anything to do with drugs, he was a real hard worker.

—Damn.

A look of alarm from the mother.

—Sorry, ma'am. I was thinking about something else. What's the problem, Pedrão?

—The guys want to know if they can start loading the meat now.

—Jesus, Pedrão, I mean really! The kid's mother standing right here . . . Jesus, Pedrão. I'm awfully sorry, ma'am, this crew has no couth, no couth at all. Now what did you say your son's friend's name was?

—Miguel.

—Do you think you could take a look and see if he's one of the victims?

—Oh my God.

Maria do Carmo, weeping in the arms of Nhanhá, the macumba priestess come to commend their souls to God, doesn't notice that the men are carting off Danival de Souza, twenty-seven years of age, black, automobile mechanic, residing on Senator Bragança Street in Mesquita, who had a job on a Dodge Dart scheduled for Saturday morning without fail, and a bullet hole in his right shoulder blade, as they load him into the black van.

—Oh God, oh my God, it's Miguel! Inácio, it's Miguel, they killed Miguel too, Inácio.

As the men lift Valtinho Sickout's corpse, Inácio raises his head, then his upper body, runs his hand through Miguel's curly hair, the last body in the line-up, his burgundy-colored jeans and that purple shirt, a bullet hole through the left arm, and the Chief asks:

—It's him? Are you sure?

—Of course I'm sure. Poor Conceição.

—Four, Pedrão, four identified in—what?—two hours?

—A record for sure, Chief.

—Someone will have to tell Conceição.

—You've got to let the press know about this. Any reporters still around?

—A couple.

—Well, shit, this is a headliner. Four of them identified, just like that, all at once, it's got to be a record.

—Sir, did you hear me? Someone's got to tell Conceição, Miguel's mother, about this.

—Of course, of course, Mrs. . . . .

The team from the Coroner's office murmur their excuse-me's, it's time to take Adilson now, and the woman begins crying again.

—Ay, my God, where are they taking him?

—Department of Legal Medicine. They have to do an autopsy, Mrs. . . . I'm sorry, ma'am, I seem to have forgotten your name . . .

—Pinheiro.

—. . . Mrs. Pinheiro.

—What about Miguel?

—Yes, and what did he do for a living?

Miguel always spent Friday night at Adilson's house making plans for Saturday, had a girlfriend named Juverci, wasn't any too bad in the ring, had a quick right, but was considering giving it up because Juverci didn't like boxing, would have gone into the service next month—the Army was very interested in him for the Olympic boxing team—had a bullet hole through the middle of the neck, problems at home because of boxing too, and a mutt who sat in the doorway until he came home at night, a bullet hole to the right of the nose, a married brother who advised him to train hard and forget what Juverci and her family said, arms covered with cigarette burns, a hematoma over the left eye, a special way of getting Juverci hotter and hotter till she just went crazy, a bullet hole in the roof of the mouth, no, I don't know the guy and I can as much as guarantee he didn't either, never even heard of this Valtinho Sickout who made a dash for it and almost managed to outrun death, who killed his friend Beiçola yelling, "God-damn son-of-a-bitch stool pigeon, piece of scum," had raped Maria Dilsa when she was just a twelve-year-old girl, killed Zezinho Nice Guy at sixteen with six shots and multiple stab

wounds, screaming, "Now hit me, you son-of-a-bitch, now just try and
hit me," with each shot, each stab of the knife, screaming, "Hit me, hit
me, you son-of-a-bitch," was buggered in the reformatory, incarcerated
at Ilha Grande, went looking for the guys who buggered other guys by
force to wipe them out, had a bullet hole in his right hand, and it was
firmly established during the investigation that Danival de Souza didn't
know him any more than he knew Danival, the mechanic who was
getting better and better every day, who in his boss's opinion had an
exceptionally good head for cars, dreamed weekly of hitting the jackpot
in the sports lottery, had screwed plenty of good-looking black girls but
not one equal to Carmo, not ever, not Carmo, who he'd won through
the joys of the bedroom, she was crazy in love with that sensual, black
rogue who'd been involved in a lot of suspicious business but was now
undeniably reformed, even the Chief had to admit that, and who had
a bullet hole in the upper section of his spinal column because he'd
stopped by the Belfort Roxo Bar to have a beer after a movie since it was
such a hot night, and had never met the guy who definitely looked like
he was from the Northeast and had a hole in his shoe, calluses all over
his hands, a dark red cotton shirt, worn indigo-blue pants, hematomas
on both cheeks, an ear dangling from his head, probably shot off, a bullet
hole in the temple, two bullet holes in his abdomen, a bullet hole under
the arm, two broken ribs, split lips, a broken tooth, a bullet hole in the
throat, and who was buried in a pauper's grave after spending a month
in the Nova Iguaçu morgue without anyone coming to claim him.

DAY TO DAY

Hélio is older than Zé Carlos and Julinho, approximately the same
age as Heitor, and has a certain ostentatious and impersonal elegance
about him, like clothing models in four-color magazines; Zé Carlos
always has more money in his pocket than Julinho or Heitor, but no one

knows how much cash Hélio carries (they rarely go out as a group except for those mysterious Friday nights, when tension and anxiety prevent them from paying attention to such things); Heitor holds his liquor better than Hélio, Julinho, and Zé Carlos, and he drinks just about anything as long as it's not sweetened, with no preference for brand or quality (on the other hand, he can't handle grass at all, it makes him throw up, and he only smokes occasionally to see if he can get the better of that shitty herb); Julinho works less than Zé Carlos, if that's possible, since Zé Carlos hardly ever shows up at the office—his father owns the company—because he's always so busy chasing young girls, but Heitor and Hélio work from nine to six (Hélio as a minor partner in a chain of supermarkets, Heitor as assistant manager of accounting for an auditing firm); Hélio dislikes blacks more vehemently than Zé Carlos, who doesn't like anything, but when it comes to choosing it makes no difference to Heitor and Julinho; Zé Carlos is the one who likes his women the youngest, once they're past fifteen he thinks they're no longer appealing, while Heitor thinks they're appealing at any age; Hélio chooses his women more for their minds and conversation (except of course at an orgy, where anything goes and the idea is to screw as many as possible, to try for a pentathlon or even a decathlon), and Julinho isn't really too interested in women, lately he's only been nailing some local beach bunny, and a couple of faggots, for money; Heitor likes soccer better than Hélio, Zé Carlos, and Julinho, who thinks you'd have to be nuts to leave the house, brave all kinds of traffic tie-ups, stand in line to buy a ticket, another line to get into the stadium, put up with the sun in your face and beer prices that are sky high, just to see your team get beat and come home cursing the referee (to which Heitor responds that there's nothing in this world, *nothing*, like being in the stands cheering when América scores a goal); Julinho likes cars—sudden acceleration, hairpin turns, tires leaving rubber around corners—as well as Hélio, Zé Carlos, and Heitor, and he's the best driver of the three (but doesn't own a car: he just "borrows" them for a while and then abandons them);

Hélio laughs less than the others; Zé Carlos was picked up and dragged in to the station once when he was caught seducing a girl in the doorway of the high school with two joints in his back pocket (a problem his father resolved with a few thousand well-distributed cruzeiros, no mention of the episode, no record, on the books), but Hélio, Julinho, and Heitor have never been inconvenienced by the police; Heitor complains more about life and rising prices than Julinho, Hélio, or Zé Carlos do during these furtive encounters once, occasionally twice, a month, when they drink hard liquor (whiskey, cachaça, vodka) and carefully outline their plans in an undertone; Julinho enjoys the beach more than the others, who only go there to look at women (though never together, except for Julinho and Zé Carlos, who have been hanging around with each other since they were kids); Hélio is the only one who drinks when he's home alone, watching movies on TV, which is something Heitor would never do because he'd rather sit around with a bunch of guys drinking and telling juicy stories, nor Zé Carlos, who drinks only on those Friday nights, or in order to give a little encouragement to a girl, nor Julinho, who prefers the white stuff; Zé Carlos likes his .38, Julinho and Heitor favor snub-nosed .32s and Hélio packs a Beffeta he bought in Europe; if he were to count the words, Heitor could claim that he reads a good deal more than Julinho, Hélio, and Zé Carlos (his reading consists of the sports, crime, and metropolitan sections of two daily papers, in addition to books and detective magazines) but Hélio's reading is more concentrated, and includes the sociology of advertising, theories on violence in society, and several books from a collection called The Great Thinkers (he intensely identified with Karl Jaspers's anguished man, but no dialog there, of course); Julinho is more of a "believer" than Hélio, Zé Carlos, or Heitor, but he doesn't think about it much, it's all just a simplification; Hélio is more a man of consciousness and words than the other three and has tried to explain that their group is pretty safe for now due to such and such set of circumstances and he can go on and on about it, but when he talks to Zé Carlos, Heitor, and Julinho about such things his words go in one ear and out the other; Zé Carlos is the cruelest of the four; Heitor tries, every once in a while, to organize a meeting of the group outside those Friday nights (perhaps this might be considered a sign that he's the coarsest of them), but the others won't even discuss the subject (by the end of the night they've had enough of each other) and one of them just says: "It's just no good, Heitor, can't you see it's no good?"; Julinho understands nearly as much about politics as Zé Carlos and Heitor, which is to say: nothing, but Hélio knows a few things about it and sides with the government; Hélio likes more sugar in his coffee than Zé Carlos, Heitor, and Julinho; Zé Carlos likes discotheques and dances more than the others, but even so he prefers private parties with more than enough girls and coke to go around; Heitor takes the kids to the beach Saturday mornings (seeing him there following the voluptuous hips of bikini-clad women from behind his dark glasses, buying his peace with ice-cream and lemonades, who could imagine he was the muscular man various witnesses reported seeing around Curral das Éguas, or Pian, or Vila de Cava, or Belfort Roxo, or on Calundu Hill, or in Marambaia, or Campo Grande, or Queimados, or Austin, or Nova Iguaçu, or Caxias, or Jacarepagua; or Mesquita, or Coelho da Rocha, or Meriti—the man they've been describing on the radio?), but Hélio sleeps late on Saturday morning or lies in bed smoking, while Julinho and Zé Carlos hang around stores listening to records or go to the beach and relax with a little acid floating around their brains; Julinho likes his girlfriend better than Heitor and Hélio like their wives, but Zé Carlos doesn't like anybody; Hélio goes to the movies less frequently than Zé Carlos, who sometimes takes in two a day: Kung Fu, porno, shoot-em-ups, and detective stories; Zé Carlos favors colorful silk shirts, Heitor and Hélio have to wear suits and ties, and Julinho is always in jeans and sneakers, he's never, ever, worn a tie in his life; Heitor smokes too much and drinks too much espresso, to the point that the others sometimes complain about his yellowed hands and his penchant for dropping everything at the most inopportune moment to go get a coffee; Julinho's favorite food is french fries, Heitor's is gnocchi, Hélio likes rare-cooked beef and Zé Carlos likes codfish with lots of olive oil; Hélio is a quieter person than Heitor, Zé Carlos, or Julinho (of the four, only Heitor could really be considered expansive); Zé Carlos's future (and escape route) are guaranteed by his father's money, which is why he's always more sure of himself than Hélio, Heitor, and Julinho when they go out on Friday nights; Heitor thinks more about the future than Hélio, Zé Carlos, and Julinho (he even went so far as to buy long-term health and life insurance), but that doesn't mean Hélio isn't a thinker—his thinking is of a different quality, he thinks about the immediate future (what it would be like if they were to get caught: the press, his colleagues at work, the elevator man, his face on TV, his wife making explanations) and this has already become a part of the fear this secret work excites in him on those Friday nights, when he comes home hiding the wet spot spread across the front of his pants.

THE REAL TRUE
SON OF THE BITCH

"they adorned theyr most shapelie and appealyng negresses in silke dresses and golde chaynes and sente them into the streets to live a dissolute and scandalous lyfe, punishing those who did not yeeld two hundred mil réis per day, and those most wantyn ones yeelded better than two hundred mil réis and savd the difference with the intension of buying theyr freedom, but often after buying sayd freedom they causd an even greater scandall, by then being muche accustomed, indeed taking pleasure, in the lyfe of pleasure."

(Estevam de Saa Perdigão—Commemorative of the Discoverie of Lost Golde.)

Ten-year-old Alfonso is a good boy, and hasn't the slightest idea he's a son of a bitch.

* * *

Elisabete, Bete, Elisa, Lisa, Maria Elisabete, the whore who bore him, is 25 years old, 5 as a hooker, 10 as a mother, 8 in the capital, 11 separated from her husband; all lies, of course. She is really 29 years old, 9 as a hooker, 10 as a mother, 11 in the capital, and 6 as a widow.

* * *

Once when Alfonso was little he saw something: a naked black man came out of her room and down the hall to the bathroom, and when he went back inside they laughed and shrieked and moaned like crazy. He had heard that people screwed; that must be what screwing was.

—Hey Mom, is it fun to screw?

—Fonso! What the—I mean, of all the stupid, idiotic, pain-in-the-butt questions! Really. Where'd you hear such a thing, anyway?

—Well, the kids say that when you grow up the best thing in the world's to screw.

—Did they say anything about me? Did they? Come on, I want to hear it.

—Not really. They said their fathers screw their mothers, Alfeu even saw them once.

—And what did they say about me?

—Well, just that I don't have a father, so you don't have a husband to screw, that's why you screw everybody else.

—I don't want you hanging around the kids in this shitty neighborhood, you hear me? It's their mothers are the ones who screw everybody in sight. You stay the hell away from those boys, or we're gonna have to get away from here. Riffraff's what they are. Who was it? Which one of those brats told you I screw everybody, come on, tell me, who was it? I want to know.

—It was Feu. Feu told me and he said he wants to do it with you too, if you do he does, 'cause he already knows how, he told me he knows how.

—Tell him to screw his mother, she's the only one who could like a cross-eyed kid with buck teeth like him.

*   *   *

—You said it, honey. Out of commission. A whole month without screwing, 'cause it hurt like hell. So I said to myself: Okay, now I'm really fucked, I've got a dose for sure. I screwed this guy, a real pain in the ass, I mean listen, I just don't like big pricks, I mean really, I hate big pricks, scare the shit out of me. But anyway I screwed this guy who was, I mean it, this big, no kidding, like that. And I can't stand it, you know, the way it pokes around in there—you wouldn't understand, but it's like you can feel it way down in the pit of your stomach, and besides it's especially bad for me, professionally, 'cause afterwards I get scared to screw, I just keep thinking how much it's gonna hurt, but this guy had it in his mind he was gonna screw and he did, and goddamn if it didn't hurt like hell, and just kept hurting all day and the next day too, I couldn't screw anybody it hurt so much. So I said to myself, Bete, you're fucked all right, got to be the clap. So then a couple days later the guy comes back pissed as hell and says I gave him a dose. Oh, baby, did I cry, I mean for real, tears running down and the works, I was just so mad and it's so goddamn unfair, and I told the guy he was the one gave it to me, I said listen, I've got a son living at home with me and at night when I have something going he stays at the neighbor's next door—he thinks I'm an artist—and can you imagine if he found out I turn tricks and give blow jobs on the street? Forget it! With him there in the house and everything, a house this size—I mean what if my boy caught the clap? and I just couldn't stop crying and the guy ended up feeling sorry for me. Then he shows me his prick, and oh, baby, a bad sore down there at the base and he was pretty raw, and I mean I'm not all that small but, fuck, a man with a prick like that, you know? So I told him about how much it hurt and he said I should get a shot of the stuff the doctor gave him, Benzetacil, they say it hurts like hell but what are you gonna do? 'Course I was embarrassed as shit at the drug store—sure, a few of the people around here know I turn tricks and there I am asking for an injection of Benzetacil—I mean a hooker with the clap, what the hell are they going to think of me? But embarrassed or not, I went there, I mean the pain wasn't going away by itself, and Raul—I'm still with Raul, did I tell you? I even went looking for him the other day, didn't I tell you? Right, 'course not, it's been a while. Well anyway, so I went to his house, well I mean I hung around the bar on the corner by his house, and he finally walked by with his wife, Christ did he turn white, white as a sheet, aahai, and of course when he did come around we couldn't screw, right, so he decided he wanted to see for himself. Now, I don't like anybody looking up my snatch, not even doctors, 'course I go to the doctor once a month like I'm supposed to, I'm not one of those scummy whores who don't take care of themselves, not me, sweetheart: I go to the doctor, I've got a national health card, everything legal, I'll show you any time you want. Anyway, Raul took a look inside me and said: Bete, you're all torn up in there, all torn up. So you see? That bastard, that prick of a guy tears me all to hell and he's got the nerve to come complaining that I gave him the clap, plus all the embarrassment at the drug store and the pain and everything. Like I said, I don't like big pricks, that's all there is to it. Just the other day I refused to screw a guy, he took me to his apartment and everything, it was a suite, you know, with a bathroom right there off the bedroom, and I had to pee like crazy and I wanted to freshen up the old snatch 'cause I just did a number in a car—that's another thing I don't like, so goddamned uncomfortable, and you can't wash the guy off beforehand, I only went because it was a regular and I knew he wouldn't pull any shit, but I can't stand leaving the come inside me, it starts to smell after awhile and I just don't like it—well, anyway, when I came out of the bathroom this guy had his clothes off already and—no exaggeration—*limp* it came halfway down his thigh, I'm not kidding! And I said: What the fuck, I'm getting out of here, and I started getting my things together, my dress, clean underwear—I carry two or three clean pairs in my bag, and a plastic bag for the dirty ones, so I was getting my stuff together and the poor guy was just begging for it, really begging, he said he'd never screwed before, can you believe it? A man more than thirty years old! And I felt sorry for him, how could you help it, 'cause no woman ever had the nerve to go to bed with him. But you should have seen it when it got hard! Really, I'm telling you, it was like this, look, like from your elbow to your wrist, no, down to here, where your fingers start, yeah, like that. Me? Screw a thing like that? Like hell! And the guy tells me he only ever gets to come rubbing between their thighs, who'd let him do anything else? It's sad, don't you think? And then I asked him if it was okay for me to call my friends to see, but he didn't want me to, no way. They would have liked to see it, I'm telling you, 'cause look, I've been on the street five years and never seen one like it, not even close. It's like he's a cripple, you know? Just like when people get enlarged balls from the mumps, or people who've got two fingers growing together like; it's awful, the guy's a sad case, he's going to have to marry some girl who's never seen a cock before in her life, that way she'll think that's what they're like and maybe put up with it, I mean who else would? And he's going to have to work fast, like I told him, 'cause with a thing like that, by the time he's fifty he won't be able to get it up anymore, it'll never get hard enough to go in. Well, where was

I? —ah, so when Raul told me how torn up I was in there I got a mirror so I could take a look myself and then I got really pissed, oh did I hate that guy. I mean I was cut from my clit all the way back, just like when you have a baby. Christ, the man cut me open with no anesthesia, no nothing. Son-of-a-bitch. It's tough enough, being in the life, I really need some cripple like that to come along and make things worse. Oh! Did you hear? They're bringing girls in off the streets now, every day. They say there's some new chief who's really got it in for hookers. How much you wanna bet his mother turned tricks? You *know* she did—and so now we got this cop who won't even give us a fucking day off. 'Course it's only overnight—we used to get at least twenty-four hours, now they're letting 'em out in the afternoon, broad daylight and there we are in our hooking clothes, tits hanging out, skin all over the place, believe me it's embarrassing. So now I carry two extra blouses, one so I'm not cold in the slammer, it gets fucking freezing in there by morning, and a summer top that at least covers my boobs, plus long pants so I don't have to walk through the streets with my ass hanging in the breeze. I mean if my son ever saw me come home like that I'd die. At night, on the job, it's one thing, but during the day's something else. You know, you go to the bakery, the butcher's, the drug store, the cobbler, you got neighbors, you even walk different! Sometimes I think to myself it's really strange. You go buy a couple tomatoes, a loaf of bread, you do the laundry, the ironing, watch a little something on TV, go shopping, talk to the kid, get him dressed for school, all that stuff, but come nighttime there you are getting fucked by some guy you never saw before in your life. Two completely different lives, that's what it is. Which is why I bring extra clothes, I can't come home in the morning dressed so skimpy like that. I've got a detective who's a regular, I could ask him to spring me when I get picked up, but he's a paying customer, so I figure I better keep my mouth shut, make like I don't even know him. With night work you're bound to have problems like that. But I'm a professional, I don't make fun of anybody, don't give anybody any trouble. You screw me for free, though, then you gotta put up with me. Did I tell you I bashed in Raul's car? Yeah, he came by the house and started giving me hell because I was standing at the gate in my nightgown, can you believe it? I told him to come on in but he just cursed me up and down, said I had no class standing around the street naked like that. Naked—me? Are you kidding? When I take such care to carry extra clothes and everything, do you think I'd stand around naked? A housecoat is what it was, he doesn't even know a nightgown from a housecoat, just 'cause it was a little short, nothing indecent mind you. You think I'm gonna ruin my image in that piece-of-shit neighborhood? To those creeps I'm a lady! So I told him if he didn't come inside I'd bash up his car and I did, I started pounding it with a stick, put a pretty good dent in the door, ha, so he hit the gas and spun out of there. It's my own man's the one I give trouble to. But he came back, he came back later. Then there's this guy Nathan, the detective, I'm going to need him to do something for me, so I already told him he doesn't have to pay 'cause I'm going to ask him a favor, I didn't even tell him what it is yet, just some detective work, investigating something that's been bothering me, I mean making me really miserable, it's a crazy thing. His name is Nathaneal, Nathaniel, they call him Nathan. But he always insists on paying.

*　*　*

—Mama, why don't you get married again?
—What an idea, son. To who?
—I don't know, just fall in love and get married, like everybody does.
—Ha, no, not me, son, not me. I hate men.

*　*　*

—I can't take much more of this, it's torture. All I have to do is look at him and I get all choked up inside and feel like crying. It's driving me crazy.

—Try to forget it, for Christ's sake.

—How can I, dammit? It's easy for you to say—he's not your son.

—But there's nothing you can do—really, tell me: can you think of anything to do about it?

—How should I know? All I know is I was lying in the maternity ward with my cunt all torn up, shot full of painkillers. And I'm supposed to know?

—Well, fuck, I didn't even know you then.

—That's right. That's right.

—Shit, Betinha, I didn't mean it that way.

—Just leave me alone, okay?

—All right, listen. I'll go check into it for you, I'll ask around.

—Take your hands off me. And forget it, you don't have to check into anything.

—I'm telling you I'll do it.

—No one asked you to ask around, I can ask around, I've got a mouth too, you know.

—Christ, Betinha, you're impossible. Son-of-a-bitch.

—Sure. Sure, Raul. But have I ever said to you—hey that's your problem? Have I?

—That's not what I'm saying, Bete.

—Have I? Answer me, damn it, I want an answer!

—Look, it's just that I'm getting a little fed up with this thing.

—Oh, no you don't. You don't come over my house and tell me you're getting fed up. Did I ever drop by just to let you know I'm fed up with you?

—Okay, Bete, okay, you're right. But just don't get so upset, okay?

—I'll get upset when I damn well please. This is my house, you don't pay the bills here, you don't put in a fucking dime. So don't think if you come over here and tell me you're fed up with me I'm going to stand around and listen.

—Look, Bete, I'm trying to help, I really am, I'm serious about this. About Fonsinho. Just tell me, what do you want me to do?

—Nothing. Forget it.

—But I'm trying to help.

—Forget it. I've got other people to help me.

—Who?

—A man I know.

—A trick?

—None of your business.

—I told you I don't want you getting too friendly with clients . . .

—Yeah? And who the hell do you think you are, huh, Raul? I don't take orders from you, sonny boy, the days of pimping are over.

—Just a little advice, that's all.

—I go around with whoever I want, you hear? And I don't need you, not even to screw, 'cause you know I don't like men with big pricks.

—Who's the guy?

—You jealous?

—Who's the guy, Bete? I'll beat the shit out of him.

—Ha, ha, listen to the big man. You know who this guy is?

—Just tell me.

—He's a detective. That's right, precinct four. Why don't you just go down there, I dare you. His name is Nathan. Well? Get moving, damn it, didn't you say you were on your way?

—Bete, Bete, don't provoke me.

—No, I mean it, go on. He's got a big, bad gun, he knows karate, judo, capoeira. It's the fourth precinct. His name is Nathaniel, but just ask for Nathan, everyone knows him. So what are you waiting for?

—You're impossible, Bete. Ever since you got it in your head that kid's not your son. Impossible.

* * *

—Well, I just ran for it when they went by in the paddy wagon, 'cause I figured they were going to stop and try to pick me up, and I ran smack into some punk, you know, with long hair and all, and he grabbed me like this with both hands, I figured he was looking for some action, right, so I said: Hey, out of the way, Bud, I'm running from the Man. And he said: Yeah?—and of course I thought he was just some long-haired punk kid, right, so I said: I'm running from the Man, you deaf or what? So that's when he really grabbed me and said: Okay, bitch. And the guy's a goddamn cop and I tell him I'm running from the Man! So he threw me in the back of the van and they drove around and around for like two hours taking corners and throwing me around back there, my head kept banging on the side of the van and I was screaming fucking son-of-a-bitch but they just kept driving around in circles and when they finally let me out I was all banged up and fucked for sure. The time before that I got picked up I was practically naked, I was wearing this dress that was really hot, I mean indecent, with my tits just about popping out and cut so low in the back it almost showed my crack, it was something else! Anyway, that other time I was lucky and they put me up front, there were so many girls in the back there was no room for any more, so they put me up front with the men. 'Course the other girls don't like it when you ride up front like that, right, and there was this scummy whore who came up to me when we got out, she comes up to me and says: Hey, you hit me in the eye. Now, how the hell could I hit her in the eye when I was never even back there with that pile of shit? Once we were in the slammer, listen to this, the goddamn whore kept on with this story of how I hit her in the eye, that she was going to cut me up and do this that and the other thing. And I think it was that time, yeah, had to be, we were in the lock-up right next to the male prisoners, bunch of crooks and no-good drunks. Whenever they made any noise the guard could come along with a big stick and he'd poke it through the bars just like that and jab at them and bash up their hands. I mean all the guards really want to do is sleep, you know? So if you let them sleep, no problem, but that bitch was looking for trouble. Jeez, I fucking hate it in jail, the way the guys in there keep asking to feel you up and stuff, and some of the girls let them. They stick their arms through the bars, there's just bars between cells, and lots of girls let them feel some tit, even a little pussy sometimes, really, some of 'em give hand jobs, they pump up and down like crazy for a while and then quit before finishing them off, all just to pass the time. Anyway, where was I? Oh yeah, so my tits were practically hanging out and there's this g.d. woman threatening to cut me up and I didn't know if I should cover up or what, I mean can you imagine trying to work—in my line of work—with your tits all cut up? I'd really be fucked. So I got ready to let out a scream, right, I didn't give a shit if the guard got pissed off, and as soon as I opened my mouth the man came pounding that fucking club on the bars yelling: Damn it to hell, what's all the fucking noise? Honey, I'll tell you he was mad, he was so mad he said he was gonna throw a pail of piss at us, they've always got a pail of piss around, you know, to stick the prisoners' heads in, so anyway, I couldn't rat on the bitch or the rest of them would have killed me as soon as he left. So I told him I had to talk to Nathan—I told you about Nathan, right? He's supposed to be on the Death Squad, his picture was in the paper and everything, something about a lawsuit—and I knew I shouldn't let on that I knew him, you know, personal, but what was I supposed to do, with that bitch ready to cut me to pieces? Well, the guard didn't want to call nobody, you know how it is, they catch hell from the top later, so of course they don't believe a word we say, I knew all about that, so I said Nathan would fuck him but good if he didn't take me to see him right away, I told him it was urgent I called it, something I had to discuss with Nathan, and he couldn't decide if he should take me or not but he said okay, but I'm telling you, bitch, that's what he said, right, he called me a bitch, the bastard, but I couldn't say a word or I knew he'd just leave me there, and he said: I'm telling you, bitch, if Nathan doesn't want to see you you'll be the one who's fucked, when I bring you back here you're going in with the men. And I go to leave and that g.d. woman says: You'll be back, sweetheart. She calls me sweetheart, just like that, you know? And the men, the men start up with hey, sexy, come over here, baby, look what I got for you, and he's holding his balls like this, right in front of the guard, and I thought shit, if Nathan says he doesn't know me and sends me back here ay-yi-yi, and I went with him but I was scared as fuck, I'll tell you. I mean Nathan's as tough as nails, he'd just as soon beat the hell out of anybody gets picked up stealing stuff, man or woman, it's like something happens to him, something comes over him. Jesus, you gotta feel sorry for anybody he gets his hands on, really. I never saw him get like that of course, but I heard enough about it, one time he went after some girl who'd rolled her trick or something, I think it was a guy he knew, too, I'm not sure. Anyway, he grabbed her and started beating on her right in front of everybody, as an example, you know, and he told her if he ran into her anywhere else around town he'd give it to her all over again, that's what he told her afterwards, and you know no one ever saw her again, I even heard she got married. 'Course I don't believe that, never knew a whore to get married, but who knows, could be—did I tell you Raul wanted to marry me? The day he got married, I was over his house that afternoon and he said: Bete, if you want I won't get married—if you want I'll marry you. But you've got to make up your mind fast because after this afternoon it'll be too late. Huh! You think I wanted to? So later he could throw it in my face that he met me hustling ass on the street? Not me, no sir. I thought about leaving the life and getting a job, I thought about it a lot. Some days it's tough, but I like it, I *like* it, you know? I even quit once, I quit the street and went home to Goiás, but my father wouldn't get off my back, I don't want you going out like that, it's too low cut, and every time I disappeared for a while he was sure I was with a man and he just wouldn't get off my back. That's the way it is in the interior, you know, for a woman who's separated. 'Course now I'm a widow but when I went to Goiás I was separated, I told you that, right? Not yet? About my husband Sílvio who died, yeah, it was insecticide poisoning. Well, he was a little thick between the ears but I adored him. Oh, he beat me like a dog, oh boy, I hated his guts for that, once I even got so mad I bashed him over the head, no kidding, he fell down real slow with his eyes rolling up in his head and I thought: Mother of God, I've killed him. Ay, I was shaking

like crazy and I ran out of there, I ran to my father and said: Pop, come
quick, I hit Sílvio over the head and I think I killed him, and my father
came running all right—no, no, first he asked me what happened and
when I told him how Sílvio beat up on me—Pop didn't like Sílvio because he was half-black, not that you could hardly tell, he was pretty light
and he was real handsome, Jesus Christ was he handsome, and Pop also
didn't like him because he went to bed with me before we got married,
you know how it is, and Pop had to watch how he treated Sílvio all that
time or else he'd split and not marry me and then I'd really be fucked and
have to become a hooker, right? So when my old man ran out of there he
knew Sílvio beat up on me, no fucking way he was going to help him, he
was gonna finish off that damn nigger, that's what he called him, Jesus
God, what a mess, and Sílvio wasn't dead after all, he was on his way over
there with his head bleeding and a knife in his hand ready to kill me,
and then my father got really worked up, he went after Sílvio with his
cattle prod—you know that thing they use to drive a cart, to poke the
oxen? And so Sílvio got all torn up and couldn't even get close to my father, and Pop was yelling if he came around again he'd kill him, and he
went over there to pick up my things, so I never went back to him, to Sílvio. 'Course I still loved him, and I was three months pregnant, even,
but we didn't live together anymore, we couldn't, 'cause he thought I was
screwing around with somebody else. And I wasn't, honey, I really wasn't,
even though I felt like it, even though I ran into an old boyfriend from
when I was twelve years old, the first guy to try to get to me, no kidding,
and the only reason he didn't end up banging me was 'cause he couldn't
get in, I must have been really small, I mean he spent a whole afternoon
trying to get that thing in me and it just wouldn't go, it hurt like crazy
and I was screaming bloody murder, to this day I can't stand men with
big pricks—I told you that, didn't I? Right, so anyway, where was I? Sílvio—ah, I was talking about Nathan. Right. So Nathan didn't look any
too happy to see me coming and I thought oh my God now I'm fucked
for good. And he was pissed when the guard told him I asked to talk to

him: Talk about what? I don't have business with prostitutes. What's the
deal, bitch, speak up. So I said: Can I talk with you in private? And he
said, just like that, Talk about what? goddamn it—waving his hand like
this, almost hitting me in the face, and he yelled: Come on, speak up,
slut! And then: You can go, Papacu. After the guard left I figured he'd
calm down, I thought he was putting it on a little maybe, but nothing
doing, the man was pissed as hell and for real. And all of a sudden I knew
what to do, and I told him he was the only one who could help me, that
it was a problem with my son, and it was true, honey, it's what'd been
gnawing at me all this time, making me think so much—me, who's got
no practice thinking, it gives me a headache, no really, I don't even know
how long it's been going on, this thing's been growing in my head, but I
just keep remembering things that happened in the hospital, and I'm
never sure if I'm imagining things or what but then I came home and
Fonsinho grew up, and the impression I had in the hospital—oh, I don't
know, everything was so confused, and my insides all torn open, and my
mother and my sister came from Goiás to live here, and the nurses kept
bringing babies in and out to nurse and I got it in my head that they'd
switched them somehow. Of course they said no, impossible, that could
never happen, and time went by and I sort of forgot about it, everybody
forgot about it. But I'm telling you, babe, it's been on my mind for over a
year now, and I told all this to Nathan, only I didn't call him babe, naturally, and I asked him to help and he said he would. For more than a year
I've been having these doubts, it's been a fucking weight on me, ever
since my mother said you know, it's funny, Fonsinho doesn't look the
least bit like you. And I kept looking at him and looking at him, and he
doesn't look anything like Sílvio either, not a bit, and I asked her if she
remembered all that confusion in the hospital and she said no. But then
there's really no use talking to her, I mean because she drinks, and I told
her straight out when she's drinking not to come around, I can't stand
the stench of cachaça. Huh. Sílvio was into cachaça too, and Pop was a
boozer, and now my mother. But I never touch the stuff. The other day

I said to myself: I need a glass of cognac, damn it, I don't even remember what I was so pissed about, I forget now, but I ended up vomiting like crazy, I threw up my whole guts. Anyway, what was I saying? About Nathan? Right. So he's looking into it for me.

* * *

—(Distraught) Tell them I'm in the theater.

—I didn't know what kind of artist you are, so I said I didn't know. *She doesn't want to talk about it.*

—(Studying his mouth) But you don't have to explain anything. Just say my mother's an artist. Period.

—But they want to know, Mom, they ask me questions. They say: Is she in the movies? the theater? does she paint pictures? And it's just that I didn't know. *I don't think she wants to talk about it.*

—(Measuring the distance between his mouth and nose, much farther apart than mine) Well, tell them I'm in the theater.

—Okay. It's just that I didn't know, that's all. What's it like in the theater? *Is it okay to ask?*

—(Studying his lips, the upper much thinner than the lower, nobody's got a mouth like that, me or Sílvio) Just like on TV, Fonsinho. We pretend we're happy, then we make up a story, we pretend we're sad, have a fight with our boyfriend, get another boyfriend. It's just a story, every day another story.

—Do they have kids in the theater? *I want to go too.*

—(Studying the color of his eyes) No, no kids allowed.

—How come?

—(Examining the shape of his eyes, the same, the color's the same too, more or less) It's X-rated. There are X-rated movies, right? Well it's the same thing in the theater. Plus it's only at night, kids have to study during the day and go to sleep at night. That's how come.

—But there are kids on TV. *She just doesn't want to talk about it.*

—(Measuring the distance between his eyes, the color's the same but the distance, no, it's much different) Sure there are, I never said they were the same. I said the theater's *like* television. Some things are different, of course, there's things you can't have in the theater. Like shoot-outs and—what else? There's the ocean, you can't have the ocean.

—Can we go to the beach, Mom? I want to go to the beach. *She promises but she never takes me.*

—(Studying his nose: no one could say *that's* like mine) We'll see, it depends on money. I'll work days a little and then we'll go.

—You can work days in the theater? You said it was only at night. *Now she's going to get mad.*

—(Studying his nose, nostrils sort of half-open, I don't have a nose like that thank God) If I said there was, there is. And besides, you ask too many questions. (Sílvio didn't have a nose like that, neither does Mama, nobody does. And look at his cheeks, so round and chubby, a little puddingface, nothing like mine, not a bit) But remember: Only if the weather's good, you hear? I'm telling you right now so you can't say I didn't warn you. I can't stand the beach when it's cloudy and windy, ugh, it's awful.

—Then we'll go to the movies. *To the theater.*

—(Studying his hair) Uh-huh. Sure. (Almost black. Mine's dark brown, at least when it's natural) And what about your homework, hmmm? How's it coming?

—I finished already. Except for there's one part I couldn't do. *She won't know either.*

—(Examining his chin, sort of an indentation in the middle, not quite a dimple—Raul's wife's the one with a chin like that) What's it on?

—Stuff about independence, why Brazil declared independence. *It doesn't matter, I like you anyway.*

—(Looking at his body, so erect, a little short-waisted) Well! I know a few things about that!

Hooray!

—Listen, it was like this: just put that the King of Portugal wanted to arrest Tarcísio Meira, he was the King of Brazil, and take him to Portugal. They wanted to be the ones to run Brazil, see, so they could take everything back to Portugal for free. So Tarcíscio Meira, who played the King of Brazil—what was his name?

—Dom Pedro the first. *She knows, she knows!*

—(Looking at his uppity little ass, shoulders thrown back: kind of like me) That's right! Dom Pedro I and Deonísio de Oliveira and Glória Menezes decided that Brazil had to split up with Portugal. And then there's the scene when a priest comes with some letters telling Dom Pedro to arrest Deonísio de Oliveira and come back to Portugal on the double, but he didn't want to so he got up on his horse and yelled Independence or Death! That's what happened, that's how it went.

—What was it they wanted to take from Brazil for free, what should I put—gold? *Ah, she won't know this one, but it doesn't matter, it really doesn't matter.*

—(Studying the way his hand holds the pencil, his short nails, thick fingers: entirely different from mine, Christ he can't be my son) Ah, I'm not so sure about that. I think it was gold, or maybe diamonds, I don't know. I forgot that part. (Watching his head nod to the beat as he writes, his slender neck, like mine, that little hollow in the back, oh God, he's such a good boy, Oh God)

—And who was Deonísio de Oliveira supposed to be, what was his name? *José de Alencar.*

—(Looking at his ears, so tiny, are mine like that? or Sílvio's? No, Sílvio's stuck out like an elephant's) José . . . José something. Oh, I don't know, I forgot that too. They called him the Minister of—something. Just put Minister.

—José de Alencar?

—(Studying his teeth: I never had spaces between my teeth like that. Oh God, I can't stand it) I don't know, it was something like that. Put

Minister, Minister of Independence. But hurry up, it's time for me to go. It's late.

*   *   *

He put on his pinstripe suit and went out. Nathan walked with the swagger of an old-time man-about-town, and he had sideburns to match, which as a matter of fact the chief had already told him to shave off, but he's just jealous. The white hair at his temples made him look like a cross between an adman and a nightclub singer; but his walk—forceful, athletic—was the walk of someone who's not easily intimidated.

He climbed the stairs to the Maternity Hospital, strode inside, and asked to speak with the director. Not in that supercilious way people talk when they're annoyed at not getting satisfaction from an underling and need to appeal to a superior, well-then-I'd-like-to-talk-to-the-director, or even may-I-please-speak-with-the-director; not him, he wasn't so easy: I want to talk to the director, and it wouldn't help matters for her to trot out any of her receptionist courtesies, may I say who wants to speak with him please, because that would only make him more belligerent, he'd pound the counter as he had so many times before and say you better just call him fast, this is police business! and sometimes he even threw in a dammit, which on that particular day he avoided since he was there on a delicate, unofficial mission, and the girl attended him right away, escorting him right this way, sir, to a room where she asked him to please have a seat, and she went to call the director, who was generally so very difficult to see.

The director naturally began by saying but sir, that would be impossible, all accounting records are burned after five years, trying to be oh-so-polite, I only wish I could help you, it would certainly be my pleasure, but all this struck the detective as a bit odd, he still couldn't decide whether to remain genteel or to come out and say: Look here, I

don't even want to know what kind of highway robbery you're into, I'm
not investigating graft, but he decided to take it slow, to chip away at
the cracks gradually, mentioning that it was quite an important case,
I know we can resolve this without a lot of bother, giving the man a
chance to weaken, making him understand he wasn't about to leave
without the information, but this guy was irritatingly sweet-tongued,
the type who anesthetizes people before he cuts them up, but not with
me you don't, buster, there's no anesthesia that'll work on me, so the
only thing to do was to get belligerent, insisting in a rather loud voice,
look here, I'm not investigating your books, I don't even want to know
how much you're stealing from the National Health Fund, all I can say
is the information I'm looking for damn well better turn up, and fast, because I know a thing or two about this hospital, that's right—how about
denial of emergency care for starters, it's a daily occurrence, how'd you
like a pile of lawsuits on top of you? And then there's the case of the boy
who was put in the morgue alive by mistake and froze to death, uh-huh,
I know all about it, I've got witnesses, so the solicitous director decided
perhaps it would be best if he went personally to find the registers from
ten years back, and with the help of two other men he began sorting
through dusty packets in a large room which looked more like a ware-
house than an archives, and found, after two hours' search, the book
with the names of the parents of children born September 30, 1968, as
well as the five days preceding and following. The most helpful director
gave his word that in fact they didn't have the addresses, admissions
forms really were destroyed after five years, believe me, we only keep
the registers, honest to God, but ever-anxious to be of help he added
that back then all hospital births were registered at the notary's office
across the street, and so Nathan walked out with sixty-three infants
and one hundred twenty-six parents to investigate, much obliged, sir,
for your cooperation. Take care, now.

*   *   *

—A real nice guy, I wanna tell you.

—Oh, Nathan, that's terrific, you're so good to me! (I can't believe it, a guy as handsome as you, treating me this way. I bet the girl at the hospital was ready to put out the minute you walked in with those white sideburns, talking real macho: Who's in charge of this joint, dammit? I bet she never saw a man like you, and I can't thank you enough.) God will reward you for this, Nathan.

Arrogant, shameless, threatening:

—Heh. I'll charge you later.

—Right now is okay with me. (Not that I've got anything to give, really, just myself. And that's yours for free, my pleasure.)

—Baby, I don't start nothin' I can't finish. And I'm not doing this for you, it's a case, that's all. I get a kick out of cracking a case, it's in my blood.

—Sure, okay. (Whenever you want me, here I am in the flesh.)

—And this is going to take some time, you know. There's an awful lot of people to check out. By the way, you can help too.

—Me? (I'll help, I'll help.) Sure, whatever you say. (I'll come with you in the car, siren screaming like crazy, and me there, in the car with you, me and you looking for all those people, for a month, maybe more, me and you looking for my son just like on TV. Some dude flirts with me and you punch him out and I say: Never mind, Nathan, I'm used to it, it may be news to you but this happens to me all the time, hookers are like crooks and beggars, no one asked us to be who we are so we're all fucked. Don't worry about me, though, thanks anyway.) Me? What can I do?

—Well, let's see . . . Your kid was a boy, too, right?

—Right. A boy.

—Which means we can eliminate all the girl babies from the list.

—That cuts it in half! (And we'll go looking for the other half, just like on TV.)

—Shit. Just give me a chance to think. Fuck. Even without the girls it's not gonna be easy. Lots of people probably moved by now, most of them maybe. Some maybe even out of town. This is some job, all right. First, we'll cross off the girls.

—You think a lot of them moved, really? Wow—just imagine. It's gonna be tough, huh? (And who'll check them out if they moved to a different town? Unless . . . yes! Unless you take a leave and we go looking for them, and sleep together, husband and wife, in the hotels. Of course we'd need some money, but I'll turn a couple of tricks and give it all to you. I know you don't want to have much to do with me, not as a friend or anything, you probably think I'll be trouble, bothering you all the time, but I won't, I know my place. You could walk right by with your wife—are you married?—and I wouldn't even look at you, like I never met you. I know my place, that's why I get along so good with everybody. It's not so bad being a hooker, you know, there are times I even like screwing. Not always, I mean certain tricks are a real pain, but it's not as if you can always pick and choose either, you know? And when we're on the road together I'll take anybody who comes along, and we'll have all we need.)

—Here we are. Twenty-eight boys to check out. Not gonna be no cakewalk.

—I'll help if I can, I really will. (Sure. What can I do, when nobody's got no respect for me—there'll be fights, yelling and screaming, I'll get in the way is what I'll do, be better if I don't go at all.)

—At the notary we'll be able to eliminate some more names. Your kid was white, you say?

—That's right.

—You sure?

—Of course I'm sure. (You think I'd have a black one?)

—So. We'll cut the black ones from the list. And if we're lucky, half the kids born in that fleabag hospital are black.

—It's getting easier already! (Kojak.)

—The hell it is. Just leave this to me, okay? Only thing you understand is cock. You know what it's like to try and locate a suspect when all you've got is an old address? 'Course not, you don't know shit. Anyway, listen, 'cause here's what I want you to do.

—Shoot. (You sexy thing you. But don't ask me to do anything too hard, *please*, or I'll screw it up and never find my son and you'll never ask me for anything again 'cause I ruined everything.)

—I'll take you over to the notary, okay, and I want you to look at the register of births day by day and write down the addresses of all the couples on this list. Don't forget to write down the district, either. And for Christ's sake don't forget to put if they're white or black, okay?

—You think I'll be able to do it right? (I'm so scared I'll make a mistake, it'll be my fault it comes out all wrong.)

—There's no way you can go wrong. Unless there's nothing but shit between your ears. I'll ask the guy at the desk to keep his eye on you. Or let him do it and you just stay there with him and wait for the list, otherwise those fuckheads will take a month to get the job done. Why the face?

—Well, what if they don't treat me right? (It's always a fight, a scene, I'm sick and tired of places like that where they don't even give me a chance.)

—They'll treat you right. I'll tell them you work for me.

(Fantastic!)

*   *   *

I can't say I don't like it. You know, you talk, tell stories, you listen to all kinds of stuff, so many things you find out about. Sure you get fed up, but that's true with anything, it's not 'cause you're in the life that everything comes down on your head. And good things happen too, like there you are freezing your ass off on the corner, pissed at life, and business is slow, not even a blow job in sight, and all of a sudden some trick you know shows up and takes you to a hotel to get warm and toasty under the covers—ah, and then you just want to stay there forever, you know? And it's good to come, too, because I'll tell you why: it warms you up, I mean it, really, it warms you up. Only once, though, 'cause you know what I think, I only come once a day—well, once in a while twice maybe—because they say it's bad for you, more than once is bad. That's what I heard, from a trick, a doctor. They say doctors are real degenerates, that's what the girls all say, but this one isn't, he's real nice, he teaches me all kinds of stuff, and he gives me sample vitamins for free. He's the one told me, 'cause I always come when I'm with him, he told me I shouldn't do it more than once a day because you lose a lot of energy that way, you lower your resistance he says, and he says I don't eat right, that's why I need to take it easy. And then he—what was I saying?—about doctors, oh, yeah—the girls say doctors are real sex maniacs, the worst. I don't know, maybe it's because they look at naked people all day long, that's what I think, you know, the way they have to examine people without being able to do anything, like a surgeon, he sees so much nastiness inside people's stomachs he just gets a taste for nastiness, that's what I think. The other day a guy asked me to piss in his face—hey, who knows, maybe he was a doctor! I should have asked. But anyway, like I said, you get to talk to people, you tell them things you wouldn't tell your friends, or your sister, but you tell them 'cause they won't be around to throw it back in your face, it's not like they have anything on you, you know, and they tell you things for the same reason. Like maybe one tells you he's had anal sex, another one tells you his daughter the coed's on drugs—is that how you say it: coed? co-ed? Who knows. Another one tells you something else, and another and on and on. 'Course there's women who don't like men, they screw for a living but don't like it, and that kind doesn't talk much, they don't do anything. I mean they do *everything* but they don't like it, and they get more and more disgusted about doing it. Lots of women can only come with other women, no kidding, lots of them. On the corner there's one, that little one, the short girl, she's like that: she only comes with women, and she likes to have a man watching, that's her favorite kind of trick. So when a guy comes along and that's what he wants, to watch, some of the girls go with her. She asked me, sure, but nuh-uh, not me, only when the street's really bad, I mean impossible, and even then I'd rather wait and see if something else turns up. That's what happened today, in fact, and I didn't go because I was waiting for Nathan to come by. I told you about Nathan, right? My friend the cop? He's taking care of some business for me, personal business, I haven't been able to work right I've been so upset lately. I'm not sure I should even tell you—oh, I guess it doesn't matter. It's my son—I have a son, you know, he's such a good boy, you should see him—but somehow I got it in my head that he's not really my son. Oh, honey, if you only knew what I've been through with this, the agony. All because of my suspicion that they switched him in the hospital after he was born, switched him for some other baby. But it's not just a suspicion—I'm sure of it now, positive. So this friend of mine, this cop Nathan, he's looking into it for me. Sixteen more children on the list to check out—sixteen, imagine. Well, by now there's probably only twelve or thirteen. He's been working on it over a month now, he asked me for a picture of my husband who died and everything—he had cancer—anyway Nathan asked for a picture of him, and you know he had the nerve to ask if my husband really was the father, I mean as if I'd have a kid from off the street! We're in the life so people think we have kids like that, without even knowing whose they are? As if I'd take that chance . . . have a baby without knowing if the father's got some disease or something, I mean he could be sick, you know. So the cop, his name is Nathan, he's looking into it for me, real detective work, he's been to Piracicaba already, 'cause he had a hunch, he was sure that's where the kid was, but he wasn't: Nathan takes one look at them and he knows, yes or no, he says he recognizes crooks just like that, just from looking at a picture once, and if he sees him on the street he's sure, never makes a mistake. They have special training, you know. Me—ha. Say I'm walking down the street and I see someone who looks like someone I know, I'm never sure if it's a john, or a neighbor, or where I know him from, I'm lousy at remembering faces. If I was in his line of work I'd be fucked. It's the truth, the street's the only thing I'm good at. I just don't have it in me to sell things, either, to work in a store or something. I tried it once. Just not for me. I'd never be a cook, that's for sure. All that mess and bother in the kitchen, food clogging up the sink, that's not for me! And there's no way I could work in an office, either, I only got to second grade and in the sticks where I come from they don't teach anything right, we didn't learn shit, not even how to type. So what's left? A factory? Mother of God, up at five in the morning, home at eight at night and you don't make shit, Mother of God! So the street's not half bad, you know? 'Course if I didn't like men, like those girls I was telling you about who hate them really, then I'd be in trouble. So I'm not so dumb, am I? What do you think? I know I'm nothing but I don't owe nothing to anybody either. The other day I was thinking, this lawyer explained to me, a trick of mine, this lawyer explained that for him to become a lawyer they had to build schools, pay teachers' salaries, I mean money for this that and the other thing. He explained the whole business but I forgot the rest. So I don't exactly know how it all goes but he said he had a debt to pay society, something like that. And the other day I was thinking, see what you think of this, I mean nobody spent a dime for me to end up here, you know, so I figure that means I don't owe anything to anybody, right? Am I right or what? What do you think? Hmmmm? A hooker is like a beggar or a crook. The reason we're fucked is because no one asked us to be what we are—it's true, isn't it? We can't get no respect 'cause we're not what they want us to be—right? I mean I don't know, what do you think? You think when I was a kid I wanted to be a hooker, when I was a little girl? You think a dirt farmer's born thinking: when I grow up I want to be a dirt farmer? Hey, I mean I doubt it. God's the one who chooses. And so the better we do whatever we do the better we are with God. And you know something, sweetie, that's why I get along so good with everybody: screwing doesn't bother me like it does a lot of the girls. If I didn't want to be the way I am then I'd have to be something else, don't you think?

* * *

—Betinha, Betinha.

—Raul, oh Raul.

—Ooooh, that's good, soooo good.

—Mmmmmmm. Sex-x-xy.

—You think I'm kidding around, is that it?

—Oh, don't get upset. I just don't like all the lovey-dovey stuff.

—What lovey-dovey stuff?

—Oh, all the mmmmmm, ooohlala stuff. If it's good, it's good, you don't need to talk about it.

—It's the life, Bete. It's being in the life that's killing you.

—Oh, fuck.

—No, listen to me, what I'm saying is the honest-to-God truth.

Naked and friends, enjoying the afterglow. Wet and sticky. They lit a cigarette and passed it back and forth.

—So, this guy Nathan, he's taking care of things for you, huh?

—Don't start asking questions if you're just going to criticize.

—No, I'm serious. Nothing I'd like better than to have this whole thing over with.

—He's still got ten addresses to check out. You know, it scares me, Raul. Thinking it's almost time, it's almost over. It's torture is what it is.

A fearful hug.

—You think he'll actually find the boy?

—Well, *he* thinks so, he says he'll find him for sure.

—And then what?

—That's just it: then what. That's what I don't know.

—Don't you like Fonsinho?

—I'm crazy about Fonsinho.

—Then give it up, forget about it.

—I can't, don't you see I can't?

—Why not? Hmm? You tell me why.

—Because it's a lie, damn it!

—Only because you think it is.

—I know it is! Not think, *know*.

—You should give it up before . . .

—Before he finds the boy? Is that what you mean?

—Yeah, before he finds the boy. It'll be better that way.

—Over my dead body. This is something I just have to get straight.

—But why, Bete?

—I just do.

—And then what? So you find him—what do you do then?

—I don't want to talk about it. Don't spoil it. I'll worry about that later, I'm not even going to think about it now. What I have to do now is find out the truth. I'll figure out the rest later on, my head can't handle everything all at once.

—I just don't get it.

—You know, it's funny, Raul. You're good to me and everything, you help me here at the house and all but, well, you don't *really* help. There are men I hardly know who help me a lot more than you do. Don't get mad, listen to me for once, damn it. See what I mean? We can't even talk. Well, today I'm going to talk, and if you want to get mad, get mad. There's lots of men who help with our problems, us girls, not just because they give us money, that's not it at all. But you know you think about something, and you talk to a john, then you talk to another one, and a sort of path gets started in your head. Plus you can learn a lot from the other girls, too. Really. There's one, a friend of mine, she rehearses what she's going to be every night before she hits the streets. Like she says: Tonight I'm going to be sweet and innocent, just like Regina Duarte, you know all those sweetie-pie parts she plays? And she puts on a real short wig she has, just like Regina Duarte's hairdo, and she's sweet and innocent the whole night, really, you should see her. Or she decides her mother just died, say, and she's just got to get to Bahia, so she stands on the corner all dressed in black, and she tells the whole sob story to all the men. She invents a different person practically every night. Now why do you think she does that, why does she need to make up all those stories?

—I don't want to hear about life on the street corner, Bete, I just don't want to hear it.

—See? See what I mean? We can't even talk.

*   *   *

He grabbed the suspect by the scruff of the neck and the seat of the pants, effortlessly heaving him into the air, yelling let's see how you like the slammer you piece of shit, swinging him back and forth for momentum, and tossed him in the back of the paddy wagon, paying no attention to the *aaaaaiiiii* which echoed from inside because he was preoccupied, I wonder if there's still time to check out one more address for that bitch, and he slammed and locked the door thinking, sure there is.

A nearby tree offered plenty of shade, but he left the van in full sun so that nigger learns when the police say stop you better stop, and strolled in the direction of the address he had memorized, looking at trees and houses, remarking to himself these folks don't have such a bad life, and rang the bell without for a minute shirking his professional surveillance of the area: this house could use a paint job, and the yard's a fucking mess, in the same rapid glance taking in the flaking paint of the door and window frames and concluding that this was the crummiest house on the block, just as he heard footsteps approaching, short, quick footsteps of a child; the door opened and he sensed immediately: it's him, look at the little bastard, son-of-a-bitch, it's him. If it had been a different house in a different neighborhood he would have just picked up the boy and carried him off to show the bitch and let her decide what to do, which one to choose, it was all the same to him, but as it was it would be wiser to take it a step at a time and find out exactly who I'm dealing with here,

so he said: Is your mother home, sonny? The boy called Mommmmmmy
and stood there waiting for an answer, it's her face, son-of-a-bitch it's
that goddamned hooker's face for sure, and the boy didn't take his eyes
off him, staring the way kids stare, if you're insecure it can make you really uncomfortable, but not him of course, he was used to it, have to do
a shitload more than stare at me to make me uncomfortable, but instead
of an answer a lady appeared: shorts, sex-on-wheels, barefoot.

Nathan wasn't the type of guy to take his eyes off a pair of thighs like
that, even when it was time to attend to serious business, choosing his
words carefully, but he knew how to think about two things at once, he
was trained to listen and interpret and listen and put everything in context, a very complicated kind of thought which in this case would have
to coexist with those hairs on her thighs bleached almost golden by the
sun, and he had already convinced her not to go back inside for a pair
of sandals and a skirt, that won't be necessary, ma'am, this'll just take a
minute, I've got a suspect waiting in the van anyway, and he made up
some story about how he had to get the guy back to the precinct right
away for interrogation so they'd be able to pick up the whole gang before
anybody realized one of the group was in the clink, all to appear more
seductive to those thighs because after all you never know.

The woman seemed a little agitated, as if she were hiding something,
listening to him say he was there on a rather delicate matter resulting
from an investigation which had been going on for some four months
and which now, fortunately or not, was drawing to a close, seemingly a
real gentleman, polite enough to warn her that she would perhaps not
find it particularly pleasant, thinking he would have taken a shower
and worn a nicer shirt if he'd known a lady like this was going to come
into the picture. So very considerate, he asked if it wouldn't perhaps be
better for them to have this discussion out of earshot of the boy, whom
the woman suddenly hugged protectively, I bet she's already figured out
what's up, and waited patiently to show what a nice guy he was, you never
know, until he saw the hand clasping the boy slacken—of course, she

was gradually understanding it all, going limp, saying why don't you go play for a while, son, watching the boy pull away, turning to face him, now she's changing tactics, she weakens and she's mine.

He got up and walked to and fro as he spoke, to show off his firm stride, all the women liked the way he walked, no, there is absolutely no possibility I'm mistaken (also demonstrating that he had no pot belly), I began this investigation right there in the maternity ward, he was going to say hospital but chose maternity ward because that clarified things even further, closer to the heart of the matter, and he saw her eyes widen, understanding, he observed her hand gesture and thought I'm gonna screw this one for sure, imagining the dark pubes beneath her shorts, that's right, I'm absolutely certain, not a shadow of a doubt that the infants were switched in the hospital. He was used to people crying, this waterfall of tears wouldn't bother him at all, it was just that she was so sexy, a real turn-on, bent over with her hands between her knees saying no no no over and over, someone could walk in any minute and ruin everything, so he strode over near her and put his hand on her shoulder, a show of support and an attempt to get her to calm down and a test to see what would happen if he leaned closer, and she did stop crying, pulling her shoulder away and coming at him in the way he least expected: So what do you want, Mr. Detective?—a lioness, he could throw her to the floor right now, and screw her—money? Is that what you want? Ferocious, a wild beast, and he continued his efforts to soothe her, madam, what are you saying, relax, please, we can work it out if we just stay calm, there must be some misunderstanding here, but he could see he was losing ground and he was pissed at himself for that. Standing directly in front of her, so that if she were interested she could appreciate his massive bulge, he told her this was not actually an official investigation, there were ways of working things out, it's just that there's this woman, nobody important, who's convinced that her son was switched and she got it in her head she wanted him back again, that's all, what do you think we should do, putting the situation in her hands, smiling a little to remember the nigger sweating it out under that hot sun and whoa!! his member began to swell.

The woman began an endless litany of her life with that boy, she seemed to be about to go off the deep end, how she always cared for him as a son, it never mattered to her if he was or he wasn't, though her husband had been suspicious and gave her trouble ever since the boy was born, but that boy suckled at my breasts! she murmured, half crying, half talking, and she squeezed her breast as she said it, sexy little tit, how she suffered for him, suffered for ten years the stares and comments of people saying, funny, the boy doesn't look like either one of you, and she didn't understand it either but what did it matter, he was her son, almost shouting *my son*, as if she could hold on to the boy with her words, she really did seem half out of her mind, and his cock was going limp again because it was one thing to try and win her over in conversation, a reasonable exchange—a phone rings in the distance—but in the midst of that madness there was no way to negotiate anything. He tried to speak, resting his hand on her shoulder again just to test the reaction, but this time she didn't even feel it, the only thing which seemed to matter to her was her own story, now she was going on about her husband, he even left me once he was so suspicious, and just as he was beginning to stroke her shoulder, no bra strap under the blouse, the boy came in and wrecked everything, telephone for you, Mommy, his eyes growing wide to see she was crying, then turning to look at the man who watched her leave the room dabbing at her eyes, the man who was thinking, Shit, what a nice piece of ass, son-of-a-bitch.

He studied the boy while the mother talked on the phone in the other room, the kid really does look like that fucking bitch, and thought maybe it would be better to forget trying to screw this broad, prove to all the women there's no flies on me, I get the job done, and they'd tell the men and the men would tell the people and the people would tell other people, spreading far and wide the story of the detective who found the real, true son of the bitch. So the thing was, he really needed to decide if one fuck was worth missing out on all that. Would it be worth saving the story just for her, being a hero just for her, which of course might add a measure of appreciation to the fuck, after all. He didn't like this delay, though, a telephone call—bad manners to leave me waiting like this, and he remembered that he had told her he was in a hurry, not that he cared about the nigger roasting in the heat, fuck him, but after all, he'd been so polite and understanding, fucking lack of consideration, shit, and he ended up getting so mad he decided he should definitely make her put out in exchange for the secret: he'd agree to tell the other mother that her son was one of the three on the list who had died, but after he screwed this one the hell with the bargain, ha! then I go and tell the bitch the whole story and still get my glory with the women, an idea he liked so well that he laughed to himself right in front of the boy, who was getting more and more upset because his mother was crying and now the man was laughing, and that was the scene she saw when she came back into the room and pulled the boy close to her, the protective lioness again, and ruined all his plans, that was my husband on the phone, and she'd told him everything, he'd be right home, fucking son-of-a-bitch.

*   *   *

She closed the bedroom door:

—I want to hear all about it.

He laughed, hung his jacket, handcuffs, and holster on the coat-hanger behind the door, and said:

—In a bit of a hurry, aren't you?

She made a face like someone obliged to be patient.

He unbuttoned his shirt, watching her with that strange smile. Opened his belt, pulled it through the belt loops, brandished it in the air and, still smiling, *ccccrack*, gave her a swat.

She rubbed her arm:

—Ow! That hurt!

He yelled:

—Take off your clothes!

She looked toward the door:

—What's going on Nathan?

He laughed out loud, like a big kid playing, and hung his belt on the hanger behind the door. Locked the door and pocketed the key. Sat down on the edge of the bed, took off his shoes and socks, and stood up again.

She just stood there, this wasn't what he'd been like the few times she'd been with him before.

He took off his pants and briefs and hung them behind the door. He laughed, looked left then right as he flexed each bicep, gave himself a hard, fast punch in the stomach, testing the musculature, looked down at her on the bed and delivered his next order:

—Suck on it.

She shrank back on the bed:

—What's going on, Nathan, you're acting weird.

He stiffened with rage:

—I said suck, damn it!

She sucked.

He waited until it was good and hard and then nearly suffocated her, jamming it down her throat with her head wedged in his iron grip, gasping for breath as he laughed, ready to yank on her hair and ears if she threatened to bite him.

She looked up into his face, startled, still not understanding the strange smile, breathless and confused with that dick stuffed in her mouth.

He let go of her suddenly and sat down on the bed roaring with laughter, watching her catch her breath.

She gasped for air, red in the face, wheezing asthmatically, and said:

—Give me the address, you son-of-a-bitch.

He went over and slapped her hard.

She screamed this time:

—Give me the address!!

He grabbed the hem of her blouse with two hands and pulled roughly, yanking it over her head. Pinched one of her breasts.

She winced, her face contorting with pain, but didn't make a sound. She tried to flail at him.

He wrapped his arm around her like a boa constrictor and said through his teeth:

—Don't fight me or I'll beat you to a bloody pulp.

She went limp.

He pulled at her pants and underpants, silent, brutish, in a hurry.

—I'll do it. You're going to rip them.

He yanked harder—the sound of fabric tearing—knocking her off balance.

She managed to fall on the bed instead of the floor.

He pulled her pants the rest of the way off, and her shoes along with them, and threw everything on the floor. Then he said:

—Turn over.

She turned over, craning her neck over her shoulder in fear, her legs dangling off the bed.

He gave her a few whacks on the ass, yelling as he beat her:

—Shameless fucking whore! Take that, bitch, piece of shit!

She still thought she could change the game, still didn't really understand:

—Ow! Shit, Nathan, that's enough for Christ's sake!

He stopped hitting her, spread her legs apart with his knees, put his two hands over her mouth, and rammed it in.

She screamed through his hands, suffocating.

He ejaculated, bellowing softly, soon after entering. Then he pulled out fast and sat at the edge of the bed, leaning back on his hands, feet flat on the floor, smiling as he watched his cock deflate.

She couldn't stop crying.

He fished a cigarette and a lighter out of his jacket pocket, lit up, leaving cigarettes and lighter on the night table, and sat down on the bed to smoke.

She turned over and sobbed into the pillow.

He exhaled in a steady stream, satisfied, smoking his cigarette down to the end. Looked for an ashtray to put it out and put it out on her ass.

She howled with pain and surprise.

—Give me the address, God damn it!

—Rudeness will only make it worse.

—Why are you doing this, Nathan? What did I ever do to you?

He got up, opened the closet, and tried to yank out the rod that held the hanging clothes. The wood snapped but wouldn't come loose. He was in no hurry:

—Nothing. What could you possibly do to me, bitch?

He took a quick look around the bathroom, came back for a chair, climbed up and unscrewed the showerhead and the pipe connecting it to the wall, climbed down and came back into the bedroom carrying the pipe and the chair. Instant reflexes: he heaved the chair at her just as she was reaching for the gun hanging behind the door.

She fell and slumped over, whimpering:

—Aaaaaai! Oh God, oh my God, now I'm really fucked, oh God what have I done?

He hit her in the face, the chest, the stomach:

—What did I say, huh? What did I say? Rudeness will only make it worse, that's what I said, isn't it? Isn't it, you shit?

She slumped further, almost flat on the floor:

—That's right, Nathan, that's right, that's what you said.

He rested one end of the pipe on the dresser and the other on the footboard of the bed, testing its strength by raising himself onto it as if it were an exercise bar. He got his belt and handcuffs from behind the door and, sticking the pipe behind her knees, suspended her between the bed and the dresser like a trapeze artist.

—You be good, now, while I go take a leak.

She heard the urine splash in the bowl, then watched his shadow recline on the bed, reach for another cigarette and light it. The backs of her knees were starting to hurt. She spoke like someone begging for something without wanting to beg for it:

—It hurts, Nathan . . .

He was calm, very calm:

—I know. People have died from it. Or been crippled.

She was quiet for a while. But shrieked loudly when he put his cigarette out right in her asshole this time. Then she couldn't stop the crying: the pain, the rage, the helplessness.

He gave her a piece of advice:

—If you let me nap a while it'll be better for you.

She tried to stop weeping, tried to cry only on the inside, in spite of the pain, the rage, the helplessness. She could only beg:

—How long am I going to stay like this, Nathan?

He stretched out his foot and ground the heel into her vulva, as if he were killing a spider.

—Who knows? Let's say until my cock gets hard again.

She waited a while, afraid of the silence, afraid of something sudden and awful in the silence.

He was getting drowsy:

—Sing something to make me go to sleep.

She hesitated.

He spoke from between his teeth, enraged:

—I said sing!

She sang: mad mad dog with the big bad bark, Fonsinho's a 'fraidy-cat and scared of the dark.

He corrected her:

—Nathan's a 'fraidy-cat.

She sang: Nathan's a 'fraidy-cat. She sang it twice, then only hummed the tune between sobs.

—Please can't I talk instead of singing? Please? I can't sing, I really can't, I'll talk real soft, real soft, just silliness and I'll talk you to sleep, okay?

He nodded agreement and mumbled sleepily:

—Sure, tell me a story.

She waited a moment and then began talking very softly, almost to herself:

—A story. Okay. Once upon a time upon a time. That's what a story is—something happened once upon a time. That's how it starts, something that was once, there once was. There's times when it wasn't, but that's not a story. Once upon a time there was a princess and her mother didn't like her and her father beat her but that's not a story it's a tale, a tall tale, which was once upon a time, the tale of the hooker who got beat up by everyone around. Of course I won't tell that tale to anybody, 'course not. Relax, don't worry, all this already happened more or less and it was once upon a time. Nobody pays any attention to us anyway, to such nonsense, and even if they did—I never told anybody about it before, why start now? That's it, go to sleep now, don't worry, whores, crooks, beggars—no one pays any attention. Besides, if you added up everything I've already gone through it would be even worse than this, it's just that it's all spread out. My father, the son-of-a-bitch, beat me, Sílvio beat me, I've had johns who beat me, boys, even women. Been to jail too. Why'd they put me in jail? Fuck, I even let them piss on me, all the stuff that's happened to me and I'm still here aren't I? So I figure there must be a reason I'm a hooker, right? There's got to be. I'm a hooker because there's people who need to screw—that's it, isn't it? So then it's not the same as being a crook or a beggar, who needs crooks and beggars? But then I don't get it why do they beat up on us, too? Does that mean we're the same? There's something else I don't get. There's people, there's got to be people, who say I'm a good hooker, just like they say so-and-so's a good doctor, like me, for example, I say Dr. Roque's a good doctor, or Zildinha's a good seamstress, so I know there's got to be people. If you do your work right people notice. So I'm thinking, look, the more cocks I service, the more times I take it in the ass or get a beating without complaining, the better I am, right? Owwww, Nathan, it hurts like hell, this stick between my knees. Oh God, is he really asleep, oh God. Doctors have that doctor-look, all in white, thermometer, stethoscope, they understand all about diseases and they pump up that thing they put around your arm, with a little pump, *tchof-tchof-tchof-tchof-tchof.* And what do we do? We stand around on the corner with our tits hanging out having a great old time laughing about getting screwed in the ass and along comes the Man and carts us off to the slammer—when we were doing everything right, weren't we? I mean I don't get it—ohhh, God, it hurts, son-of-a-bitch—I'm thinking about one thing and then I get off onto something else, I'm all mixed up. Oh, fuck, it hurts. Owwwwww! Aiii, Nathan, for Christ sakes take me down from here. I know why you're doing this to me, Nathan, I do. It's because I know who I am and I'm not fucked by it, it's because I know everything they do to me is a bunch of shit and you've never seen me once wave the white flag, that's why. Some people don't know where the shit's coming from, but I do, and that's why. Oh fuck my knees hurt. You know what I'd like, you know what I'd like sometime when I'm with a man is I'd like him to be the hooker and I'll be the man, oooh, I'd really stick it to him. I know it's impossible, never happen, it's just some nonsense in my head, but that's the way I think sometimes. Oh my God. I know, I see clear as day that's the way it's gotta be, or else everything would get all fucked up, so confused nobody could understand what's going on. But they should realize, they've got to realize they— owww, shit—they need me to be a hooker. Or else what'll happen to me? Christ, Nathan, I can't take it anymore. Things are bad enough I mean bad enough already and just when you need all the help you can get along comes a son-of-a-bitch like this to make life hell. Nathan! Tell me the fucking address! You hear me, you fucking dog, you S.O.B.? Nathan! Wake up, Nathan! I'm gonna be a cripple! Fuck, I can't even feel my leg any more. Oh, shit—Nathan! Hey, Nathan! Fuck!

He woke up mad:

—What the fuck do you want?

—Take me down, Nathan. It hurts like hell.

He smacked her hard on the ass with an open palm.

—Who said it was time to wake me up? Now you're gonna be sorry.

She made her excuses:

—But I'm going to be a cripple! I can't move my leg!

—Sure, sure, I know.

She was moaning.

He dug his fingers into her leg, her feet, and said:

—A little bit longer.

She was begging again:

—Take me down from here, for the love of God, Nathan. He crouched above her and began to rub his flaccid cock back and forth between her legs.

—If it gets hard, you come down.

She tried to help, squirming as much as she could, and moaning from the pain.

He liked this and got hard right away. He laughed.

She sighed.

—Thank God.

He tried to go inside her but she was swaying back and forth. Holding her by the waist he entered her, even though it wasn't the greatest position.

She reminded him of his promise, weeping, fearful:

—Fuck, Nathan, you said—

He punched her in the kidney yelling

—Shut up!

at which point his cock fell out. He shoved it in again, this position really was lousy, his legs were getting tired. So he picked her up, throwing the pipe on the floor, and carried her—still tied up—to the bed where he lay her down, rammed it in her, bit her, took it out, slapped her, pinched her, put it in the rear, threatened to strangle her, took it out, bit her, cursed her, hit her, spit on her, rammed it in again, panting, starting to bellow softly, and then letting out a prolonged roar, he came inside her.

She waited until his convulsion was over, roused herself from what felt like death, and demanded firmly:

—Now give me the name and address.

He was exhausted, no longer caring to resist, and told her everything: names, address, and all.

* * *

In.

You think I'm good? I mean, you know, like people say so-and-so's a good soccer player, you think I'm good? I am, aren't I? I mean I do everything right, don't I?

Out.

I've got to go talk to that woman. Just the idea of it scares me to death. She doesn't know I work the street of course, uh-uh, she doesn't know anything about me. Now that the time's almost here it's driving me crazy. Five or six months, I can't remember for sure, that whole struggle to find the boy and now I get weak in the knees just thinking about it. How am I supposed to say to her: I want my son? Attorney Francisco says she knows her rights and all—Attorney Francisco's my lawyer, I pay him and everything. But how can I just go there and talk to that woman?

In.

You know the beggar who hangs out on the corner across the street—you know, the corner where the girls all stand around, it's the next one down. The guy's filthy, I mean he looks black he's so dirty, only he isn't, he's white, at least his belly's white, and you can see his cock when he pisses and it's a white guy's cock. Anyway, he sits there staring at himself in the mirror, sometimes he just sits and stares. Well anyway he really gets to me because I look in the mirror a lot too, you know? Whenever I walk past a mirror or glass I look at myself, in all the rooms I look at myself. Well it really bothers me, I keep wondering if I'm going to go crazy like him. So then I figured it like this: it must be that he keeps looking at himself to see how fucked up he is, because I mean it can't be to see how good-looking he is, right? No way, couldn't be. Unless it's to see if he's doing a good job at whatever he's got in his head that he's got to do. It makes me cry sometimes, baby, honest, I'll tell you. God in heaven, if my son turned out like that . . .

Out.

I've got to talk to that woman, got to take care of this real soon.

In.

That's why I figure we're not the ones who choose. I'm sure of it. Positive. Beggars either, they don't choose, or crooks. Crooks are worse, of course, taking other people's things, that's not right. Believe me, honey, I really hate crooks, the other day, I'll tell you, I was so mad I thought if I catch this guy I'll kill him. He took me to the hotel, and he seemed okay, like a regular guy. He even paid in advance. But that was just it, honey, it was all part of the scam, and it wasn't until later that I realized why, that it was part of his plan to pay up front, listen to this. He paid me, balled me just fine and all, and then, it had to be when I left the room, when I was inside washing up, he went into my pocketbook and took all my money, I mean every last bit of it, and he acted perfectly normal, calm as can be, when we left together, and of course I didn't have to look in my bag or anything because he already paid me—see what a fucking scam?—and he took me back to the corner as if nothing had happened, and split. Well I got so pissed when I found out what happened I didn't even screw the next trick when I got to the hotel and looked in my bag. I could have killed that guy. Anything that belongs to somebody else is sacred as far as I'm concerned, baby, I've always been like that, since I was little. The other day this drunk came along, nobody I knew, never saw him before, and I don't like drunks, right? I told you, right? My mother drinks but she stays away from me with that reek of cachaça, she knows she *better* stay away. And anyway I was really busted, had to pay my lawyer, Mr. Francisco, who's looking into a few things for me, and this drunk wanted to go to the hotel and I didn't have any other tricks lined up, the street was really dead, so I went with him. A fat guy, I mean like this, look, like this. And so we screwed—fat guys do it on their backs, did you know that?—and he didn't get up afterward, he went right to sleep. Oh, and I forgot to say—before getting in bed he put a pile of money on the night table, stacks of hundreds, five-hundreds, I mean a shitload of dough. And then the guy falls asleep, and I was nervous as hell with all that money and I couldn't leave, could I? All I have to do is leave him there asleep and somebody comes and steals the bum's money and it looks like it was me. So you know what I did? I stayed right there and went to sleep too, mm-hmmm, I left the girls on the corner waiting for me for dinner, I stood up Raul, and all because of this drunk's money. The next day he gave me a thousand extra, that was nice. I say what belongs to somebody else belongs to somebody else, that's what I always say. And if a person ends up a crook, or food for sharks, like me, it's because somebody made them that way, that's what I say.

Out.

You know that beggar I told you about the other day? The one with the mirror—was it you I told? You know you talk to so many people—it *was* you? Right. Well, I've been thinking: maybe he looks in the mirror so he can see something else. I mean we're all stuck in this life of ours and we can't remember any more how we were before we turned into what we are now. Maybe the mirror is so he can look and see if it's still really him in there.

In.

Fonsinho? Sure he's a little suspicious. He feels something, he's so clingy lately, it's really getting to be a problem. And me crying all the time, oh, honey, it's all so mixed up, why me?

Out.

Tomorrow I'm going over there to talk to that woman. Attorney Francisco said it's got to be tomorrow, he made an appointment for me.

In.

There's so many things I've done in this fucking life, I get dizzy just thinking about it. The truth is I can't take much more of it, you know what I mean? Thirty years young and I look old already. Sure I do, of course I do, I can see it every time I look in the mirror, especially in the daytime, I see it. And even if I don't look old I feel old, from all the things I've done. There's people who don't do all what I've done even in eighty years, and I did it in thirty. And now what's left for me to do? It's all over.

Out.

I'm terrified of that man, terrified. All the dirty things he did to me. But the worst thing is I'm getting to hate men, I mean actually hate them. I'm scared of getting just like the girls around here, the ones who go around petting each other just because they're mad at men. Not me, please God, I don't want to go to bed with a man without liking it, like they do. Life's bad enough without that, can you imagine? I mean really. You know what he does, he comes around here, he pretends nothing happened, and I shake like a leaf, I don't know if it's rage or fear, whenever I see him I start shaking. It happened, it just happened, I can't talk about it. I needed a favor, he was gonna do me a favor, but it didn't work out, that's all. And now everything's so mixed up in my head, him and my life on the street, 'cause if I wasn't in the life he wouldn't have fucked me like that, and it's all mixed up with Raul too, see, I mean if I don't like big dicks why'd I hook up with a man with a big dick, and then there's my son, too, that's a real problem, you can't imagine, Mother of God, and you know I just started thinking I can't take it anymore, I just can't. Who knows if there's other men, even tricks I know—I mean didn't I know Nathan? Wasn't he a regular john and all?—sure he was. And if he did what he did, then other men could too, and I bet they do, you know? I just can't stop thinking like that: one way or another everybody does the same thing to me as he did, and how can I work thinking like that, I mean how can I?

In.

I mean I just can't take it anymore. It's killing me is what it is.

Out.

Hi, my name is Maria Elisabete Camargo da Silva.

*   *   *

—So then you know all about it, right? Attorney Francisco explained everything? *More or less.* (What do you mean more or less?) —What do you mean? He said he explained it to you. *Yes, of course he explained it to me. From your point of view. But I spoke with our lawyer also.* (Oh God, Mr. Francisco.) —Oh? And what did he say? *Well, he gave me some in-structions and he said that our conversation today isn't definitive* (Oh no? What does that mean: definitive?), *that it's just the first contact, and that I shouldn't agree to anything I feel is unfair.* (And what about me?) *Those were his instructions.* (What about me? What do I do?) —Mr. Francisco explained that to me too. So you know everything—about the case, about everything then? *Yes, of course. Of course I do.* (Yikes! That's the end of that.) *Because of that brute that was here.* (Mr. Francisco?) —Brute? Attorney Francisco? *No, not Mr. Francisco, no. The one who came the first time. A sleazy type* (Nathan?), *from the police.* (Nathan. What did he do? Attack the woman?) —Ah, him. (I'm going to have to do some-thing about this, just thinking of that man gives me the willies. Change the subject.) —So, what do we do now? *I don't know. What do you think?* —Me? Ummm, I don't know. That's what I was wondering myself. *But you came here, you went looking for him. You must have some idea, Mrs. da Silva.* (Do I? Mrs. da Silva, get that! "You must have some idea, Mrs. da Silva"!) —Well, I'm not sure. I came to talk to you, to see what you think. I think, well—what I mean is, I'd like to see my son. I mean, that's the first thing. I'd like to see him. I've been looking for him for over six months, not counting the years I just thought about it. So would that be okay? Do you think I could see him? (Mr. Francisco said I could, he said I had a right to see him. If she doesn't let me I'll tell her that, right to her face.) *Yes, yes of course you can.* (Thank God.) *But you just want to see him, right?* (See him, take him. What do you think—you can order me around?) —I don't know, I'm not sure about anything these days. And what about you—wouldn't you like to see Fonsinho, too? *That's what he's called, Fonsinho?* —Yeah. Alfonso. And yours? (Mine?) João. (Hmm, just like my father. Awful.) —That's a nice name. My father's name. *Really? What a coincidence. Imagine.* (So do I get to see him or not, damn it?) —Well. Is he around? *I'll call him. It's just to see him, right? Or else it could be traumatic.* (Like he'd turn into a fag? Traumatic, dramatic, that what she means? Oh who knows. Wonder if he'll look like me. Better if he looks like Sílvio, Sílvio was handsome. But what do I do when he comes in? Hug him? Say: My son! Should I say anything? Oh God, here he is, oh he's cute! What do I say?) —Hi João. (Oh God it's him, it's him, what relief, it's him, it's me.) *Say hello to the lady, João.* (It's him, my God, it's true, after all this time.) *Hi.* —Hello João. (Hello, son, my baby.) *Go on, give the lady a kiss, João.* (Oh God no, I'll cry, no kisses, I can't start crying. Oh silly me, I'll scare the poor kid out of his wits.) That's right, give Auntie a kiss. (Auntie my ass. She wants to steal him from me all over again. But I won't let her, no, not this time, I'll never let him go. God in heaven, he looks just like me, I wish my mother could see. His hair's straighter but everything else, everything else is exactly the same. Oh, just look, I'm scaring the kid with all my tears, or did I hug him too hard? Oh help. Help me, help him.) *That's a good boy, now you can go play* (Thank God), *Mama needs to talk to Auntie some more.* (Auntie my ass.) *Say good-bye now.* (Funny.) *Bye-bye.* —Bye, son. (I said it, I said it, *son*, my son. Funny, the way she treats him like a little kid. Fonsinho isn't like that, and he doesn't look much like her either. Must look more like the husband. Maybe there's a little of her in him, but not like João and me. Now she's going to sit down and ask me what I want again, and I don't even know myself what I'm doing here. I'd like to just take him with me, keep them both, him *and* Fonsinho, the two of them playing together, the three of us.) *He really does look a lot like you, doesn't he?* —Yes, I think so too. (Nice of her.) *And my boy, Alfonso* (you mean mine), *does he look like me?* — A little bit. Would you like to see him sometime? (No, no of course you don't, fuck why did I say that?) *Hmmmmm, well, no, I don't think so. I'd really like to of course, but I promised my husband. We've thought about all this quite a lot, we talked to a psychologist, and a lawyer, and we decided it's best to do what they suggested. You see, we've had a lot of prob-lems—even before we found out the boys were switched. My husband sus-pected it wasn't really his son.* (Ha! You mean suspected you cheated!) *I'm telling you all this so you'll understand we've had our problems too, a lot of them, do you understand?* —Right. Of course. *And so we decided that it wouldn't be good to see the boy, not for us or for Alfonsinho* (Fonsinho) *and it might even have bad repercussions on our relationship with Joaõ.* —You mean you think my coming here could be bad for the children? (Oh God.) *No, no I don't think so. You've been very nice about the whole thing. We just don't want to get Alfonsinho involved in all this. So it all depends on what we decide to do.* (She already knows what she wants to do, she's got a husband, a psychologist, oh fuck. Careful with this woman!) —Well, it's just that I can't tolerate a lie. No, hold on a minute, I mean it, this is something I discovered about myself and it cost me plenty, cost me a beating just to be here today. (My God, that's it: I'll kill that man!) Lis-ten, tell me something: if you and your husband died in an accident, God forbid, would you let me have Joaõ? *Well, he's already close to my mother and all . . .* —Would you? I'm asking you. *No, no, I wouldn't. I'm sorry, but I don't like lies either. I think it would be better for him to stay with my mother.* —Well then I'd have to fight for custody, go to court. (Fuck her.) *You could do that now* (she knows), *but you know as well as I do that both boys would suffer for it.* (No I don't want that.) *As long as you don't like lies, you'd better think about that too.* (Yeah. She's got a point. Changing mothers, at his age, would be rough on him. But what am I supposed to do—nothing? Find him and then that's it, it's over? Is it still a lie after all these years, or is it the truth by now? Am I the mother of two boys, or one, or none? Son of my belly, son of my life—which one's my son? How can I leave him here with her when I know he's mine? And how can she leave hers with me when she knows what I am? She does know, doesn't she?) —Doesn't it feel a little strange for your son to be living with someone else? Someone you don't even know? *No, not really. In my heart the boy who lives here with me is my son.* (And that's that? That's that. So that's that?) —You don't know what I do, what I am, do you? *Yes, I do.* (Holy shit!) *I know very well what you do.* (Oh, fuck, what now? Did Mr. Francisco tell her, could he have gone over to her side? Oh damn. How much you want to bet she scoped it all out, she knows where I live and everything. She's probably already seen Fonsinho, knows all about him, of course, or else she wouldn't be standing around so relaxed, she probably even talked to him, on the street, God in heaven maybe she's been to his school, how much you want to bet her husband's already picked me up, part of the investigation, that's why he's not here now, it's got to be, or else it was Nathan, that son-of-a-bitch, who told her. I've got to get free of that man. But what now, what do I do now, dear God?) —Well, what if it's the opposite, and I'm the one who dies, would you take Fonsinho for me? *Of course, of course I would. I'll take him right now if you want.* (Sure she would. That's what she wants, isn't it? Isn't it? She wants him, too. And now there's just one thing I've got to do, just one more thing. I've got to keep my wits about me so I can take care of it. I've got to make sure there's someone to take care of Fonsinho, because my mother, God forbid, and her cachaça. I don't want my son to end up a beggar or a crook. Okay, so that takes care of it, end of discussion, end of visit— the end of the story. See you later, lady, don't worry, everything's just fine.) —Fine. I just wanted to straighten a few things out. So now I'll be on my way, all right? Everything's just fine. See you later, okay? *But . . .* —See you later. Just fine. (I'll ask Mr. Francisco to arrange everything, it'll be all set, I'll be free because I'm going to kill that man.)

THE TOWER OF
GLASS

"*as a curative, complet severitie ought be demonstrated towards whatsoever revolts of sayd negroes, from floggying at the foot of the pillorie, to the most severe, that is, hangyng and quarteryng in the towne square, for terror and example, as and accordyng to theyr sentences declard.*"

(Estevam de Saa Perdigão—Commemorative of the Discoverie of Lost Golde.)

There were protests.

They gave every child a ball and time to play with it. The children learned incredibly complicated moves and some of them even traveled the world demonstrating their fortuitous dexterity. (The problem was that many of them, the majority in fact, couldn't get the hang of it, and at night, as adults, they were dark, and frightening. It would be better to just arrest them all, some said.)

There were protests.

They raised the price of meat, lifted price controls on grain, and instituted low-interest loans for farmers. So what did the farmers do with the extra cash? Well, let's just say—bah, who cares!

There were protests.

They cut salaries (which unfortunately caused an increase in the incidence of robberies) because we need to fight inflation and, as you know, when salaries rise above the index of productivity there is a highly inflationary spiral, such that blahblahblah.

There were protests.

They outlawed protests.

And so hate was born, and took the place of protests. Then came the Tower of Glass, to put an end to the hate.

The earliest glass prison, now the interior kernel of the present complex, was constructed on the site of a brick building which had once served as police headquarters. Since that was before the Grand Advancement, the original glass was of the old-fashioned sort which lacks the extraordinary quality achieved today—glass whose transparency itself is invisible: only the absence of wind blowing through the space suggests the presence of glass—an invisible pane which obstructs and impedes—and displays.

The Master Architect initiated the transformation with one quick stroke: plates of triplex glass were installed to replace the freestanding concrete wall between the street and the front of the building.

(Huh? A picture window—here? the people on the outside wondered as they passed by.)

Next they substituted glass for the walls along the side streets.

(Good grief! You'll be able to see everything!)

Then they dismantled twenty meters of the building's facade, and the first exposed rooms appeared.

(Whaaaa??!)

For a month construction halted. People on the outside would steal a glance now and then, wondering if the renovations had been completed, never daring to stop or stare as they passed by; the people inside went on with their work, though with a certain constraint, keeping as much as possible to the section protected by brick, trying to call as little attention to themselves as possible. The departments exposed to view were Communications, Wiretapping, Records, Administration, and Storage. It would have looked like any bureaucratic public agency if not for the weapons room completely visible along the left wall. Even though the glass was bulletproof, this arsenal was guarded by sentries armed with machine guns.

During the month's delay the Intelligence Section undertook a thorough investigation of neighbors, passersby, passers of rumors, this one and that one, this that and the other one. The Directorate agreed that the glass was an ingenious idea, brilliant in theory, but still they hesitated. With the impatience of the enlightened, the Scientist presented facts, photos, films, tapes, and reports urging the immediate initiation of phase two of the GPP (Gradual Pacification Plan). He played back a tape:

"I can't hear with all the construction across the street. Talk louder."

"Is there a new building going up over there?"

"No, well . . . I'm not sure. They're doing renovations on Headquarters, putting in picture windows or something, I don't know."

"Picture windows—what for?"

"Your guess is as good as mine. They do what they do, you think I'm about to go over and ask?"

"Right. Better to keep your nose out of it."

(Click.)

"So what's going on over there, anyway?"

"I don't know, really. I mean I walk by here twice a day but still I can't figure out what's the story with these windows."

"I bet it's just to show they're working, don't you think? A little P.R., that's all it is."

(Click.)

"You know what I heard?"

"No, but I wouldn't keep staring like that if I were you, pal. I heard they take your picture."

"So? I'm not doing anything, just looking. What do you think they're up to, hmmm?"

The Scientist turned off the tape:

—We have a whole month's worth of observations, recorded and analyzed. Absolutely no risk is indicated, not one in a whole month. A new concept of human behavior is being born right here in front of us, and still you hesitate?

The Directorate authorized the next step: an architectural project involving substantial horizontal additions to the building which would require expropriation of two or three blocks of neighboring houses, completion of the first glass cell, and initiation of the pilot experiment with one carefully chosen prisoner.

The first prisoner to be exhibited was young, black, simply dressed, looked rather perplexed, and had darting, agitated eyes. He had most likely been there in prison for some time; he walked with a slight limp and appeared docile, obedient, and frightened. The prisoner's day was observed discreetly.

He rose early, a little before six. Sat down on his bed, hands between his legs. (Was he cold?) He watched the people who passed by beyond his glass cell, beyond the side courtyard, beyond the glass which had taken the place of the concrete wall along the sidewalk. Once in a while he rubbed his hands together, squeezed them between his legs. He rocked back and forth gently, front to back, as if cradling a baby. He got up and knocked on the door. Waited. Sat down again, hugging his arms tightly around his chest. (He must be cold.) He stared out the window and yawned for a long time, hunching up his shoulders and hugging himself even more tightly. Then he began to jiggle his legs, faster and faster. He stood up and did a sort of halting dance in place, as if tied up, and again knocked on the door. As he waited he walked about, bouncing and shaking. The door opened and he left. Soon he was back and sat down again, seemed to be watching people pass in the street. Then he stood up, concentrating visibly, opened his arms wide, and began doing calisthenics. Suddenly he froze, arms extended, intimidated by a passerby's gaze. The prisoner's arms fell to his sides. He sat on the bed again, head lowered, rocking back and forth, cradling himself. The door opened and he was given bread and a liquid of some kind in a tin can. The man ate very slowly. Then he lay down and remained motionless for about four hours. (He must be sleeping. Life of Riley.) He woke with a start, sheltering his head with his arms, realized he was alone—yet completely exposed and sat up again, hands between his legs, head hung low. His shoulders trembled slightly for many minutes. (Was he crying?) He lay down again, on his side this time, knees drawn up close to his chest. Small tremors shook his body off and on. Each time he exhaled, a round vapor mark appeared on the glass wall and was enlarged by the next breath before vanishing. The man's hand began to trace small circles on the clouded glass. More purposeful now, he drew a five-pointed star with one continuous stroke. Another star, and another. He shifted position slightly, cupped his hands to the glass and exhaled into the cone. Then he paused, looked around, and made a signal to passersby watching him discreetly from behind dark glasses, neighbors peeking from slits of windows. A woman stopped and stared. He stood up, breathed out as hard as he could, and began furiously writing numbers on the glass. Before he could finish he had to stop and exhale again because the numbers would begin evaporating. His agitation made the woman nervous; she couldn't understand what it was he wanted. He hastily scribbled a series of numbers, some of them mirror images readable from the other side, others not; the end result was an incomprehensible mess of digits upside down, backward, correct, all superimposed on each other, and rapidly fading. The woman walked slowly away, mumbling to herself and shaking her head. The young prisoner kept tracing on the glass, as if for practice. He couldn't quite manage to complete whatever it was he was trying to do. (Must be a phone number.) He sat down. He cupped his face in his hands and stared out, glassy-eyed, unseeing. The door opened, a man stuck his head in and spoke to him. The prisoner shrank back, cringing, and replied; the man spoke to him again with threatening gestures, and he shrank back even more. As the man entered the cell the boy turned quickly and gave the glass a hard kick, with no result. The man laughed, said something else, pointed to the people in the street, then grabbed his arm firmly and led him out the door. The cell remained empty for the rest of the day. Around dusk two men brought the prisoner back, supporting him under each arm, and laid him down on the bed. They turned on the light. He didn't move. They brought food—an aluminum plate and a tin can. Still he lay motionless. They left the plate and cup on the floor near the head of the bed. He didn't move a muscle, not even to shield his eyes with his hands. Late at night they brought a blanket. In the morning he was gone.

The Scientist turned on the tape:

"Hey, look, there's a guy in there."

"Don't stare like that, maybe they don't like it."

"Then why did they put him there, in front of everybody?"

"How should I know. Come on, keep walking."

"I don't get it. I just don't get it."

(Click.)

"Sure, I'll pick you up, no problem. But I really think—hey look, you can see the prisoner in there, see?"

"Wonder what he did."

"Who would know."

"Yeah, they never tell us anything. So, anyway, are we really going to Santos on Sunday or what?"

(Click.)

"Mom, hey, Mom, look. Somebody came in, another guy came in."

"Where? Let me see."

"See him? What's that he's holding? Looks like a mug."

"How am I supposed to see, if you can't?"

"Yeah, it's a mug. A mug and a piece of bread."

"The poor kid."

"Oh, Mom, what do you mean, the poor kid? You know him or something?"

"Don't pull the curtain up so far."

"You know what he did to end up in there?"

"I just think about their mothers."

"Look, the other guy's leaving."

"Poor kid must be hungry."

"Poor kid. You don't even know him."

"Okay, okay. I'm going to do some picking up around here, forget the poor kid. Just as well. And you better watch what you're doing with that curtain, you'll get us all in trouble."

(Click.)

"If it's a number he's trying to get across, why doesn't he just hold up his fingers?"

"Maybe nobody would stop to watch. It would be too obvious."

"Too obvious? And what he's doing now isn't?"

"Plus, people are scared, you know? Nobody's going to stand around right in front of headquarters talking sign language with a guy like that."

"What do you mean? Why not?"

"Why not! Then you do it. Go on."

"Nah, not me. I don't like niggers."

(Click.)

"They're just like children—take them away from their mama and they cry like crazy. Well, I'll come by tomorrow to give him his shots."

"Okay, thanks."

"Can you see the prisoner today?"

"Oh yeah, he's in there. In such bad shape, though, you've got to feel sorry for him."

"So what do you think he is—a thief or something?"

"Nothing good, that's for sure."

"Yeah, you've got to have done *something* for them to start messing with you."

"But shit, this guy is in bad shape."

"What can you do? Nobody wants to play the good guy like in the movies."

(Click.)

"Not a damn thing worth watching on TV. Some shitty movie."

"So you're in bed already?"

"You bet—with wool pajamas and two blankets."

"How about going out for a glass of wine or something?"

"Not me, not in this cold. Listen, what's doing with the prisoner over there?"

"Well, let's see, I went by at—well, I went by a little late today, he was already lying down. They left the light on, I don't know what for. Maybe it's so they can see what he's up to from far away. But it doesn't look to me like that guy's going to be doing anything any too soon. And they brought him some food, and a blanket—last night he slept without one, imagine. But he didn't even get up, that's the thing. The food just sat there, he didn't touch it."

"What's the deal, anyway, putting a prisoner in there with no explanation in the media, no nothing? I mean it's like colonial times or something—it's like the pillory."

"I bet that's it exactly—it's like the pillory. Makes sense."

"Careful. I heard they listen in on conversations."

"Oh, bullshit. That's right out of the movies. Besides, I doubt we have the technology for that."

"I wouldn't bet against it."

"And so what if they are listening? They don't have anything on me."

"Maybe not, but the way it works you're fucked until you can prove otherwise."

"You mean *we're* the ones who have to come up with the proof?"

"Look, are you really going out in this cold?"

"Not if I can't get anyone to go with me. Maybe something better will be on TV. If we're real lucky."

"Well, take another look at the guy, okay? and fill me in tomorrow."

"Okay. *Ciao*."

(Click.)

"Stop. Come on, don't."

"Why not?"

"There's people in there, see?"

"Where?"

"In there, behind the glass."

"Aw, honey, the guy's asleep."

"Well, what about the guard?"

"He's half a mile away!"

"No, stop. I mean it. Let's go back around the block."

"But then your mother'll call you."

"So?"

The Scientist turned off the machine:

—Naturally, this is just a selection of the material. You will find the complete transcript included in the report. And there's nothing, absolutely nothing problematic. The most interesting parts are merely more of the same. In my opinion we can, in all security, move on to the next phase. That is my request to you gentlemen.

They inaugurated ten more glass cells.

Transparencies:

v as in visible

venereal visceral

vertigo vitriol

versions of vertical

volt and voltage

the virgin's vagina

the curve of the vortex

visible vice

vitreous visions

reversing the voice

the ventriloquist speaks

the veneer of the near

the inviolate glass

Twenty-five persons self-immolated in bonfires of hate, five severed their veins and bled to death in front of the glass wall surrounding the compound, three used dynamite to blow themselves into a million pieces against the glass, and more than fifty died trying to scale the wall, singly and in groups. As they arrived with their little gallon containers of gasoline, urgent in their hate and determination, a clamor of nos would rise up from the people there watching the prisoners.

Useless. Those who came to set themselves on fire were deaf and blind to the horror: they would sit down facing the glass, drench themselves with gasoline, muttering threats to anyone who approached them, strike the matches and burn to a crisp without so much as a scream. The first of them got through his whole pantomime without anyone realizing what was happening, until the moment of the match and the no! The gestures of the ones who came after him had a terrible, inevitable quality. But nothing seemed to alter the rhythm of the Tower of Glass: the arrival, turnover, and who knows what else of the prisoners. The people who came there to open their veins and let their blood run black with hate would first chain themselves to a tree, in order to make it harder to be given first aid; then they shouted, "Murderers, murderers," and quickly slit their wrists, legs, and throat. No one from inside the Tower of Glass ever got involved in these events, with the notable exception of the time a young passerby dipped his hands in the horrible blood of a suicide and wrote "Murderers" on the glass wall. Several men emerged immediately, gave chase, caught him, dragged him inside. The ones who blew themselves into a million pieces seemed to prefer the middle of the night when nobody, or almost nobody, was watching the prisoners: they would make a dash for the wall, lit fuses in hand, and a terrible scream would echo through the night just before the explosion. By the time people began passing by in the morning, new panes of glass were already in place and hardly a single splinter of hate was to be found. The ones who attempted scaling the glass wall would fall dead as the *tatatatatatata* of a machine gun split the darkness. During the day when a sudden scurrying indicated that some crazed person or group was about to try something, the bystanders scattered; all they heard, breathless with fear wherever they had dashed for cover, was the *tatatatatatata*. With time and lack of results the suicides became rare. And then stopped altogether.

The Scientist:

—All as it was foreseen, you gentlemen are well aware. They have acted just as we expected. Today we can say with certainty that we are in a position to stimulate, direct, and suppress primary behavior. And now we commence work on the fine tuning. All signs indicate total victory over Hate within a maximum of three years. Today we appeal to you to authorize an audacious step forward, and I would ask for your complete attention to my argumentation and to the piece I am about to read to you. This following is a newspaper editorial which was censored by the Opinion Control Section. I'm going to read only the most important passages. (Clears throat) "The most reactionary groups of the vast and rarely comprehensible range of interests which characterize the Powers That Be have succeeded in creating a new barbarity in the etymological sense of the word; they have created a Picture Window Prison, a shopping center of humiliation, their most recent, and we would hope last, aggression against society. We are talking about a real barbarity, and not without premeditation: only if we go back to the times of Attila, the Vandals, or the terrible Avaros, who crushed the Holy Eastern Empire under the hooves of their horses, can we find another example of such iniquity. Could it be that we are living through an era similar to that in which the proprietors of the land—who were at the same time the commanders of the armed forces and the Counts of the Kingdom—were only able to save the peasants and the cities, threatened by hordes of barbarians from Eastern Europe, from total ruin by exercising the terror of the state, thus preventing the barbarians from establishing themselves? Since these counts and the King himself were barbarians, lords of barbarian peoples who had just recently managed to organize themselves as a state—that is, a group of men living within a territory under a set of laws—they adopted in war the same methods as their enemies: terror. Are we, then, returning to barbarian times? It is sad to think we are." I'll omit a particularly verbose section and continue with the following: "The tradition of punishment by example in the public square and the exhibition until death of the criminal in a pillory harks back to those times in which humanity was fighting to create what was to become modern Europe. Was this the only way it could have been done? It is not for us to *judge* history, but rather to reflect upon it and learn from it. Was this the only way to act? It is sad to think so; it is human and Christian to think not." Leaving out another small section, it goes on: "What modern-day Machiavelli—in order to advance history one notch further—inspired this new creation? What diabolical political scientist dreamed up this fantastic glass penitentiary, which somehow escaped the brilliant philosopher of *The Prince* who, in chapter seventeen, discusses whether it is better for a ruler to be loved or feared?" Forgive me, gentlemen, please, for going on, but this fondness for prescriptions from the past is so very characteristic of the comments of the press. In any case, after some more nonsense disguised as ancient rhetoric, we come to the finale: "If the Powers That Be have one remaining shred of respect for the people of this nation, then it is up to them to explain this latest decision; to prove that they are acting with humanist, Christian motives; to prove that they are acting in the interests of the Fatherland and the Family." The end. Of course at first glance the piece seems to be an irrefutable condemnation of our Gradual Pacification Plan: barbarous, arbitrary, inhuman, Machiavellian. But I ask you: is there one substantive idea in the midst of all these adjectives? And further: if we had need of an opponent to legitimize us, could we do any better than to write an editorial like this one ourselves, covertly? The article accuses us of "aggression against society." Of course! A fundamental point of the whole project is that our aggression be visible, unlike the dungeons of old—*those* were barbarities. The writer speaks of the "terror of the state." That's the point exactly. The old words, the old liberal ideas—won't those very values of corrupted liberalism guide the state to its destruction? War is a practice the newspaper itself justifies by saying that only the use of barbarous methods saved the peasants and cities, perhaps even modern Europe itself. Basically, the people behind this editorial agree with us about who should be on top and who should be on the bottom; it's just that they don't want to *see* the aggression, they're bashful, they've got weak stomachs. The article mentions humanity's struggle to create what became modern Europe—of course this smells of historical determinism, which I don't accept, but that's beside the point—and also the pillory, and asks, very distraught, if this is the only way they could have proceeded. But do you see? It's the *means* which make them uncomfortable, the *methods,* in that they are un-Christian and/or inhuman. But what the devil is inhuman? Everything man does is human. And Christian? Why, the Church itself employed the very methods we use today and the Church is still considered Christian. As for Machiavelli, the comparison only flatters us. To summarize, then, I submit for your consideration the following: we stand for the truth, that is the principal idea in instituting the GPP. That's the reason the walls are made of glass, damn it! Excuse me, excuse me, gentlemen, please, I . . . forgot myself. Well then, what we request is the liberation from censorship of news and commentary regarding the Tower of Glass. We want the sentries abolished. And we want it to shelter not just thieves, murderers, pickpockets, and dissidents, but also razor-wielding homosexuals, angry prostitutes, insubordinate blacks. The Tower of Glass must be known by all, must be the conscience of all. The people are hungry for the truth, they want to know and to see. The Truth, gentlemen. I ask that you make this truth known throughout the entire nation. With the help of the press.

They removed the sentries, suspended censorship of criticism of the Tower of Glass, and inaugurated the first deposition rooms.

Transparencies:
variant visuals
verso and recto
the tearing of tears
on her thigh in her eye
in the eye of her thighs
member dismember

in the blue of the bruise
the pubic is public
limbs heavy as lumber
the wounds are unwound
and thus all the fuss
the invited voyeur
the reign of the pane

The Scientist turned on the tape:

"I'm telling you they don't care."

"Still, you don't have to stare. Look all you want, but you don't have to stop."

"Don't be silly. What do you think the glass is for? It's to look through, for Christ's sake."

"I don't want to know what it's for. I'm not going to stand here and stare and that's all there is to it."

"Fine, then go on home, damn it. Ah, Marta, not here—what are they going to think with you standing here crying? They're going to fucking think you've got someone inside! Marta! Shit, let's get out of here. Fast."

(Click.)

"It's like that every day. They wake up one of the guys in the cells, look, there on the right, and bring him into that room. Some of them yell at the guy, the others write stuff down."

"Do they beat them?"

"Well, it's really no big deal in there. They slap them around a little, then they say a few things, the guy talks, they write down what he says. Sometimes they take the guy inside there, and then sometimes he comes back, sometimes he doesn't. Sometimes they carry him into his cell and he just lies there."

"And it happens every day?"

"Every fucking day. Sometimes more, sometimes less. When they first bring the prisoner in the van they keep him on the inside, in the part you can't see. Then one day he shows up in one of the glass cells. They don't put them in the cells the same day they arrive, though, because some days no vans come in and still a new one appears. That's what I've figured out so far, anyway."

"And they just let you watch like that?"

"At first I wasn't sure. Then when nobody said anything, I figured I could just keep on looking. Today a guy from the newspaper even asked me for an interview, he wanted me to explain how it works and all."

"So they arrive, they stay inside there a while, and then what?"

"Well, I think—I mean no one told me this—I think that inside there is the secret part, where they have interrogations and stuff. After they've found out everything they want to know, that's when they put the prisoners in the glass cells over there, see? And then they just bring them back if they need to ask them something else, or to write down what they already said. That's how it goes."

"You mean it's worse on the inside?"

"Mmm, no doubt about it."

"Why do you stand around here watching everything, anyway?"

"Oh, I don't know. I just like to know what's going on. When I was a kid I always used to do things like take clocks apart and dissect animals to see what was inside. Curiosity. I guess I'm just curious."

(Click.)

The Scientist, enthusiastic:

—Absolutely terrific, don't you think?

(Click.)

"Naturally they're trying to prove something. (This is a professor who lives across the street, said the Scientist, without turning off the machine.) Like that diabolical machine in Kafka's *The Penal Colony*. What is it they want us to understand—if we want to stop the machine that's what we have to find out. In Kafka's novel, as the needles of the apparatus engrave the criminal's sentence on his body, he gradually comes to understand his crime, and he dies happy, relieved at having understood. Because for *Homo sapiens* it is a terrible thing not to understand something. It's the worst thing of all."

"Get yourself picked up, then you'll find out."

"No fear of that. I'm just an old decadent."

(Click.)

The Scientist:

—By the way, that reminds me: we need to be very careful with certain artists. Art employs the same method we do; perfection of form can both disturb the public and disguise sleights of hand. But emotion without scientific control, suspense, ideas, can turn people into time bombs of unrest, we'll have explosions going off all over the place.

(Click.)

"He disappeared about six days ago. We've already looked everywhere—hospitals, the morgue, everywhere."

"How awful. And they told you he was here?"

"They didn't tell us anything. I came to see if he turns up behind the glass."

"It's hard, I know how hard it is. Sometimes they take them out of the glass cell and don't bring them back, sometimes they're back the next day. There's no pattern."

"And I live so far away . . ."

"What does he do?"

"Drives a cab. And he helps a lot around the house too. But it's tough for me to come here more than once a day, and I'd have to stay and watch all day long, wouldn't I? To be sure? If only I knew he was here I could relax a little bit, keep up hope. Losing days at work, it's hard, I don't know what to do. Two days I've been here already without seeing anything."

"At least I know mine is in there."

"You've seen him?"

"Not me personally. But a friend of his saw him and told my husband. He's in there all right."

"So you're sure."

"Uh-huh."

"Well, that's good at least."

"I wouldn't exactly call it *good* . . ."

"What I meant was just finding him must be a relief, you know what I mean?"

(Click.)

"Look at that, it's outrageous. Three hours that guy's been standing there without being allowed to lower his arms. They can't get away with this."

"Yeah? What are you going to do about it?"

"I don't know, something. Form a commission, talk to people, complain to the papers."

"The papers already reported stuff like that, it didn't make any difference. Except that even more people come to see. "

"Fuck, take a look at that, I mean just look. That's bullshit."

"You're right. Outrageous. Imagine if some guy's mother was here watching something like this."

"And they say it's worse on the inside."

"If that's possible."

"I read it in the paper. That's just the deposition room, no big deal. Interrogations happen inside where you can't see."

"Just as well."

"What do you mean, just as well?"

"You know what I mean. I mean, I don't know, some things it's better not to see. I don't know."

"You want to hear something?"

"Sure."

"You said imagine if some guy's mother was here. Well, yesterday one was."

"Shit, no kidding? Is she here today?"

"No, they took her away. She fainted and they took her away."

"They took her inside?"

"No, it was a relative I think. She was standing there screaming my son, oh my son. But I don't think they can hear inside, just like we can't hear them. So then she fainted and they took her away. Somebody told me about some other woman who had a son in there; he said she threw a rock at the glass."

"Did it break?"

"'Course not. It's supposed to be bulletproof."

"What happened to her?"

"That one they took inside."

"I heard they really can hear everything we say out here."

"Did they keep her in there, is she in there now?"

"I don't know, the guy didn't say."

"I heard sometimes they turn up the sound of the mothers crying so the prisoners can hear it. That's what I heard."

(Click.)

The Scientist:

—What's important here is this: it's obvious that they don't know how to act because they're not sure what they're dealing with. All they really want is to understand. They know we have a motive and that's a good sign, an excellent sign. I would ask you distinguished Directors to notice in this proposal that I am recommending the necessity of taking a big step; I propose that we knock down the expropriated houses, raise to three hundred the number of glass cells, and construct a glass shelter for the prisoners' relatives. This last is a new idea which, added to the original project, serves our Final Objective perfectly. Its function will be to separate the relatives from the simple spectators, so that the inevitable emotion expressed by the relatives doesn't upset the others, doesn't get in the way of assimilation. Seen through glass, this emotion may even prove to be of help.

In thirty days, working around the clock, the project was completed, with new, even more perfect glass: much more durable and more transparent. Along the two side patios of the main wing of the building, facing the cells, were the shelters for relatives: horizontal corridors of glass midway between the bystanders and the prisoners. The spectators could see anguished fathers, distraught mothers, confused brothers, weeping girlfriends, loyal buddies wandering up and down the wide hallways of glass—a continuous and repetitive pantomime—in their confined search for the fortunate misfortune of sighting their dear one. Several people at once would rush toward the glass across from a cell where they thought a new prisoner might have appeared: they would look and look and then one by one go back to pacing the corridor, their anxiety one drop heavier from each new failure. It was impossible to know, when a group ran toward the same cell, whether they had been directed there by some electronic signal; perhaps it was just a matter of them advising the others that a door was about to open, bringing someone new or taking someone away; perhaps there had been some small sign recognizable to those conditioned to the novelties of the place. Once in a while an actual reunion took place: hands on this side of the glass, hands on that side of the glass, four meters separating them, and not a sound. A pounding on the glass, gestures, a prisoner motioning for his despairing father to go on home, or a mother and son who just stood and stared at each other for a long, long time, resigned. In the women's wing, mothers and daughters were afraid to look at each other for long, perhaps because each knew what the other was thinking.

Transparencies:
the form unforms
the force deforms
the lid lifted up
the wire unwinding
the flower deflowered
the tearing returning

shut in shout out
the pair in despair
breast without rest
untidy the tit
the accused accuse
the torque contorts
the tie that binds

The Scientist turned off the tape:

—Perfect, don't you think? And today, in addition to the taped selections, we have a new editorial, with another theme which may be of help to us. This is a passage from near the end of the piece. The owner of the magazine writes: "Simão Bacamarte. I'm wondering if the name of this illustrious sage, scientist, and humanist will have reached your ears in the midst of the diffuse mass of names and dates learned in high school. It's a story from the period of the Monarchy. Dr. Bacamarte constructed a big green asylum called the Green House in which he first incarcerated the stark-raving mad. Then he incarcerated the potentially curable madmen. Next, in an effort to delineate the precise boundary between insanity and normality, he also locked up the eccentrics. By that time he realized there were more people locked up than there were on the outside. And since, logically, the majority must be considered the norm, the scrupulous scientist freed the prisoners and locked up everyone else, that is, he incarcerated the small number of people who were theoretically without mental defect. Then, by instilling various abnormalities, he cured them, and finally, recognizing himself as the only perfect man in the city, locked himself up in the Green House forever. This story, one of the eminent Machado de Assis's best, is instructive to us at this moment in history. In my perplexity and indignation, I would merely like to recommend to those responsible for our Glass House, better known as the Tower of Glass, that they save the nation time, money, and the anguish involved in modem therapy by skipping a few stages and locking themselves up now, once and for all, in their glass madhouse." Now, gentlemen, aside from the obvious petulance, for which we will find a remedy, I'm sure, this article contains an idea worthy of our careful examination: where does normality end and insanity begin? The author anticipates a point I had already intended to raise here in the form of the following question: who should be incarcerated? Our work so far has identified, along with the elements which should clearly be eliminated or incarcerated or rehabilitated, a type of prisoner we did not exactly intend—the someone who may know something about someone, the wife or daughter we make use of during interrogation, the someone who knew someone but we're not sure still does, the relative or friend who might just know something—in other words the large body of people who are of temporary interest to us and have caused severe problems of overpopulation in the Tower of Glass. So I ask you: who should be imprisoned? Only the insane, the people who truly have no limits? Keeping in mind our friend Simão Bacamarte, that limited definition represents timidity, represents hesitation, and we must not hesitate. We must show that there are no limits! We must make it clear that all insubordination will be punished! That means the teacher who, instead of teaching, doubts; the artist who, instead of painting beauty, paints ugliness; the philosopher who, instead of thinking, talks; the worker who instead of producing, argues; the housewife who bangs her pots and pans together to make noise instead of making dinner; the student who doesn't study—in short, everyone who fails to produce, who is suspicious, troublesome, and intractable, should be put away! Therefore I request your authorization for the following: freedom for the insignificant prisoners and prison for the troublemakers. The prisoners who are set free will make public a great deal (of information about our experiment. And we should immediately begin construction of the five additional facilities foreseen in the project. Other states are already clamoring for their fair share.

They gave up a non-virgin bride to a smiling bridegroom a tooth-

less lady to two crying children an old man on crutches to an old man
with a beard a young guy with a limp to a woman screaming for joy a
sleepwalking boy to a terrified woman a young girl with her legs open
to a man in dark glasses a girl with burned breasts to nobody a kid with
uncontrollable legs to a corner of sidewalk waiting for someone a man
with his head hung low to nobody waiting a man with a broken rib to
a smiling family a man with frightened eyes to a very relieved woman
a young girl running to a young girl crying a child to a doctor a boy
walking slowly to a corner of sidewalk expecting someone a teenage boy
with bruised wrists to a strict middle-aged man a girl running scared to
the mother and doctor trying to catch her a man with a burned beard to
three happy-go-lucky kids a boy to a woman a pregnant woman to a man
with two sons a cheerful miss to a boy with a dog a man on a stretcher
to an ambulance a shadow to light a guy supported by a woman with
cigarette burns on her face to a middle-aged couple plus another man
a priest to an archbishop one thing to another thing one other to yet
another some things to other things.

Transparencies:
the ugh of slug
the ah of the father
the face defaced
the ow of now
the out of shout
the kick of the prick
the root of the brute
file in fall out
enough of the rough
the arc of the spark
the ire of the wire
the reach of the screech
the rite of might

The Scientist turned on the tape:

"What do the women do when they have to pee, with it all see-through like that?"

"They make a circle and surround the person."

"You've seen them?"

"Sure, but I told you, you can't see anything. They hide each other."

"Jeez, you'd think they could leave at least one in a cell by herself so we could see something."

(Click.)

"They've been letting people out for about ten days now."

"What's going on, do you think?"

"The newspaper says they're the relatives. The real hot ones they're keeping inside."

"What's the story with that guy?"

"They released him, he's been sitting there on the sidewalk for nearly a week, waiting for someone to pick him up."

"Is he hurt?"

"Looks like it. We told him he's free now, that he should get out of here, but he says he can't, not by himself. Somebody offered to give him a lift but he said no. So we give him food now and then and he just sits there, quiet like that. I guess he's waiting."

"Maybe we should call someone for him."

"The problem is he can't remember who. He says the name just about comes into his head, he's on the verge of remembering, and then he goes blank."

"Why doesn't someone take him to the hospital?"

"Because he doesn't want to. He says if he leaves they'll never find him. He says it's here they're going to come looking for him some day. Every once in a while somebody takes him to the bathroom, then they bring him back and he just sits there, sort of stretched out."

"What's his name?"

"That's just it, he doesn't know. It comes into his head but then he goes blank before it gets as far as his tongue."

"Memory problems. I had a cousin like that, he used to forget everything. He was a baker. Every once in a while he'd ruin a whole oven full of bread, completely forget to take it out."

"Does this guy remember what he does, or did, for a living?"

"Says he's a lathe operator. At least he thinks so."

(Click.)

"Yesterday they let a real pretty girl out of there. She couldn't walk too well, though, sort of dragged one leg, like this. But it could have been congenital, who knows."

(Click.)

The Scientist:

—How about that? You see, gentlemen? Things are moving right along.

(Click.)

"Let's get out of here, Mom. I'm free, so let's just get going."

"But what happened to you, son? Oh my God."

"Just keep walking, Mom, what are you doing stopping? Come on."

"Tell me! I want to know! I'm going in there, I'll march right in there—"

"Quiet, Mom, calm down. Don't make a scene. We're just gonna get the hell out of here, okay?"

"But how did this happen to you, talk to me."

"I fell, Mom, that's all, I fell. Now let's go. And you better keep your voice down 'cause they've got microphones everywhere, they'll bring us right back in. All I want to do is get out of here, fast."

"I'll sue them, I'll sue them for what they did to you!"

"Sue them! Mom, oh Jesus, let's just get out of here, okay?"

"I will, I tell you, they can't get away with this, oh no, just look at you, God in heaven. Where does it hurt? Are you all right?"

"Just give me a hand, Mom, there, that's it. Ohhh. Now start walking, hurry, okay? Just start walking."

"What's everybody staring at, so many people and no help at all. What are they here for, what did all you people come to see? To see this?"

"Never mind, Mom, it doesn't matter. And keep your voice down."

"The boy can hardly walk, he's hurt bad, can't you see?"

"Never mind, Mom, everything's fine, okay? And for Christ sakes, keep your voice down. Just put your arm here, that's it, that's all you have to do."

(Click.)

"Well, actually, it's the first time. I came down from the Northeast to see what it was like."

"Don't you have one up there? I thought they built one up there too."

"Pretty soon. It's supposed to be almost done anyway. But it'll never be as big as this one."

"You have any relatives in there?"

"Me? No—God forbid. All my people are good as gold."

"Yeah, me too, I just come down here once in a while to have a look. Saturday, Sunday, when there's nothing to do, I come check it out."

"It's funny, you know? With them inside and us out here watching."

"Only at first. It really is a beautiful building, though, don't you think?"

"Gorgeous."

(Click.)

"So they eat in there and everything, huh?"

"Everything. Each of the cells has a toilet and shower. When they go to the toilet they stand around in a circle shoulder to shoulder, so you can't see. Especially the women."

"Is it always so crowded?"

"Yup. People getting released all the time, too, but more going in."

"And out here on the street—is it always this crowded?"

"You bet. Packed."

"Hmph. Pretty wild, huh?"

"After they started talking about it on television, on the news, even more people started coming. You should see how jammed it is on weekends."

"People got to do something, right?"

"Yeah, what are you gonna do? Plus, it's free. You spend less than at the airport."

"My kids are always begging me to take them."

"Kids always like airplanes."

"Yeah."

"Plus, it's better. For the kids."

"Oh, no it's not, I don't take them any more. I heard a doctor on TV say it's bad for your ears."

"What is?"

"All that noise, they say it's bad for you."

"No kidding?"

"Really."

(Click.)

"There's times in the morning and afternoon, depending on the position of the sun, when the glass gives off a reflection, even though it's still transparent. And you see yourself inside there, you see a reflection of yourself in there with the others."

(Click.)

"A hot dog and a soda, please."

"Same here."

"What kind of soda?"

"No, I mean a hot dog."

"Boy, am I starved."

"I read in the paper the other day they torture them in there. Can you see anything?"

"Torture? You mean actual torture? No, not really, that I haven't seen. Once in a while you can kind of see into the rooms in the middle section there, I guess that's where they take down the depositions, and you can see a few punches maybe, a little cigarette burn, or somebody getting their nipple pinched, that kind of stuff. But not really what you'd call torture, nothing like that."

The Scientist:

—Now is the time for the grandest step of all. As you see, the structure is completely in place. We are ready to show them everything. From the inside out. The moment is now!

The crowning jewel, cut and polished at last. Eyes glazed over by such crystal beauty. The shameless virtue of china-closets: to exhibit and to shield, to offer and to withhold, to give and to take away. From certain angles you can see through the whole building at once glance—no brick, no cement, no whitewash: just glass and steel. In time, the spectators learned to distinguish the categories of residents of the Tower of Glass into layers of transparencies: relatives, already-interrogated prisoners, prisoners being interrogated, staff in their apartments. Such was the structure, once complete.

Transparencies:
    Transparencies:
        Transparencies:
           Transparencies:

v as in visible
    variant visuals
        the form unforms
           the ugh of slug

venereal visceral
    verso and recto
        the force deforms
           the ah of the father

vertigo vitriol
the tearing of tears
the lid lifted up
the face defaced

versions of vertical
on her thigh in her eye
the wire unwinding
the ow of now

volt and voltage
in the eye of her thighs
the flower deflowered
the out of shout

the virgin's vagina
member dismember
the tearing returning
the kick of the prick

the curve of the vortex
in the blue of the bruise
shut in shout out
the root of the brute

visible vice
the pubic is public
the pair in despair
ile in fall out

vitreous visions
limbs heavy as lumber

                breast without rest
                        enough of the rough

reversing the voice
        the wounds are unwound
                untidy the tit
                        the arc of the spark

the ventriloquist speaks
        and thus all the fuss
                the accused accuse
                        the ire of the wire

the veneer of the near
        the invited voyeur
                the torque contorts
                        the reach of the screech

the inviolate glass
        the reign of the pane
                the tie that binds
                        the rite of might

The Scientist:
—The tide of this one is "The Hypnotized Nation." I'll take it from the top: "We, who by definition and mission are interpreters of the social reality and whose job it is to make plain to our readers the confusing events of the human struggle, find ourselves for the time being as incapable of understanding as is the nation at large. All of us saw it on television: a crippled man, obviously maimed by the treatment he received in the Tower of Glass, witnessed daily by all, being presented to the nation as

healthy. Clearly the intention was to demonstrate that after undergoing such cordial treatment he was perfectly fine, perfectly alert. No wonder intelligence fails us, logic abandons us. Why deny on TV what all can see as clear as day through those most perfect windows of the Tower of Glass? There appear to be two coexistent realities here: we are perplexed because they don't fit together. What is this Tower of Glass, then: a theater? a monumental spectacle in continuous showings, robbing rating points from television series, even during prime time? There is some diabolical mechanism at work here, some fantastic illusionist blending magic with reality. We, the spectators, are paralyzed, like a frog before a snake."

The Scientist raises his eyes, smiles his wonderfully modest smile and turns the page:

—The same newspaper contains an interview with a British sociologist. Says he: "I believe that what we are witnessing in this instance is a collective search for health. Like any living organism, society avoids illness by creating a system of antibodies. And in the context of the extreme anguish to which this society has been subjected, the search to delude oneself can be seen as a search for health; to pretend not to see is to refuse to enter into their game. This society would not, after all, be able to face these facts and remain healthy, would not be able to know what it knows and keep silent without sliding into a phase of deterioration and decline; and, finally, it would not be able to be so controlled if it were not already deteriorating, feeding on anguish at the gates of the Tower of Glass and tranquilized by television." Wonderful, wonderful! It's the same thing seen from a different angle, and the angle is not what interests us but the thing itself. Very good. We can change the chronogram and jump ahead to the next-to-last phase, Attenuation and Indifference. And in the end, when everyone has perceived the metaphor, we will still have one small but definitive ace up our sleeve.

The Scientist forces a laugh and most of the Directorate laugh along with him. He removes a small piece of paper from his pocket. Eschewing improvization for the first time, he reads:

—Gentlemen, I have reached the end of my usefulness. Not long from now all you will need is a good warden. I would like to take this opportunity to express my gratitude to you for creating the ideal conditions under which Science could develop this program to its fullest. Your names shall be inscribed in History. I am grateful also to the sponsors who, in spite of their anonymity, saw that we never lacked for funds. History will undoubtedly reserve a place for their disinterested Idealism as well. Thank you. Thank you all.

They announced via all means of communication that new glass, yet more perfect and more transparent, would be installed in the external walls. It was prohibited to touch them. The renovation procedures were broadcast on national television and radio, as well as being described in detail in the news media. The nation watched as workers carried away the outmoded, outclassed panes, perfect though they were, and loaded them onto waiting trucks and, their hands protected by thick rubber gloves, unloaded the wondrous, new, invisible replacements, installing them with care and efficiency; the workers came two by two, almost collapsing under the weight of the new glass, fitting them into the frames in the steel structure, as another duo performed the same pantomime up ahead, and another, and another. In three days the work was completed. It was prohibited to touch them.

The Tower of Glass became the subject of a prime-time series; it was a frequent topic of popular opinion polls on television, in which people answered the classic question: "What do you think of this or that?"; it graced the pages of fashion magazines as an "extraordinary backdrop for extraordinary fashions"; and, finally, like a church or a tree, it blended into the landscape. Occasionally someone would get up in the morning and say: Hey, how about going to the Tower of Glass tomorrow?—as if suggesting a trip to the planetarium.

All alone in his glass room, the guard guards. Watches, listens, tapes:

—Taping in progress. Silence please! One, two, three . . .

"Oh God, dear God, what have I done to deserve this suffering? And I thought I was doing everything right, I always tried to give her the best, the very best we could afford—didn't I, Ernesto? Remember how I pounded the pavement finding the right school for her? We sacrificed so much, oh God in heaven what did we do wrong? My poor baby, my sweet thing. Every pain she feels is my pain too, every wound of hers is a wound of mine. But why, Lord? Where did I go wrong, how could I have allowed her to sink into such madness, what could I have possibly done to drive her to it? I taught her religion ever since she was small. Ernesto looked out for her as much as he could, isn't that right, Ernesto? There was none of this business of sleeping with her boyfriends, no sir, and it's so common nowadays. She was always just so, always fresh and clean, playing volleyball, all dressed in white. And now she's disgraced herself, and disgraced me in my suffering, and there's nothing I can do but watch and wait for them to send her back to me, cured. I swear I'll watch over her and protect her, yes with every ounce of our tenderness and our suffering, I'll never, ever again leave her by herself thinking such nonsense. Now is when she needs us most, she needs the strength of her family. Ernesto, there she is, Ernesto, take a good look so you'll never forget, I know I won't. You have to be brave like I am, Ernesto, and look—that's what we made, it's our error they're correcting. Don't think for a minute I'm not hurting as much as you are, you can't imagine the pain of a mother who has to hit her own daughter. You don't know what I'm talking about because you never wanted to lift a finger for her, I know you, Ernesto, you're such a banana, you're even more guilty than I am. Not that I'm saying I had nothing to do with it, of course not, I'm guilty too, I'm here aren't I? That's right. And I bet she knows exactly why we're here."

(Click.)

"Mr. Nelson, would you please explain to our television audience the difference between this special new glass and the common glass we're all acquainted with?"

"Well, common glass is a fusion of quartz, in the form of washed white sand, with sodium carbonate and lime. Now, for the kind of glass used in kitchenware, like Pyrex, the mixture is slightly different; you add sand in a base of dioxide, silica, and boron. But this new glass—well, of course I don't know the formula, but as transparent as it is I'd imagine it must have a lead base, and its strength and resistance to heat and shock suggest sand with a base of aluminum. So you see, though I don't know the precise formula, I would say that if it is in fact glass it's certainly not local. That's for sure."

(Click.)

"See what I mean? Just look, from here—see? Standing here it looks like I'm there, inside. Sometimes it's like I'm the one being interrogated, other times it's like I'm doing the interrogating, the beating, or whatever."

"Hey, you're right, look at that!"

(Click.)

"No, I just came by to take a look. What about you?"

"Me? I came to see my son."

"Oh, what did he do?"

"What are you talking about—he works there!"

"Well! A VIP in the family, eh?"

(Click.)

"I think about what torture it was when there were walls instead of glass, we didn't have the slightest idea what was going on in there. Just the not knowing, not being able to see your son or brother or father, could drive you crazy, you had to go running around to lawyers, judges, newspapers, it was unbearable. Now it's all so clear. People can watch and cry and suffer along with them, it's like visiting someone in the hospital who is critically ill. They look so small, so pathetic, because there's nothing they can do."

"Yeah. Well, enough of this heavy stuff. Let's go have a cup of coffee."

(Click.)

"Hey, you know these guys have got some fucking smarts."

"That's for sure. There's a lot of good people behind this, I'll tell you. The detail! I mean this business of reflections, they really did some job."

"You mean how when you look at it, you see yourself inside?"

"Yeah. With this new glass in the outer walls it's incredible. Perfect. Those guys must have studied everything there is to know about theories of behavioral reflexes, the boomerang effect, and all that shit, you know? Researched the whole thing."

(Click.)

"The presence of drug-trafficker Valtinho Sickout among the five dead in Baixada Fluminense, that is, the presence of a known criminal, even a gangster, sentenced to over thirty years in prison, in addition to another suspicious character presently under investigation—these facts clearly establish that this killing is one more episode in the continuing gang drug war."

(Click.)

"He's looking at me again. We never saw each other before in our lives, and now he knows I'm here because of him. Of course it's for me too, that's what it's all about. The obligation I feel to look at him, to look after him, I don't know, it's making me crazy. Any minute now they're going to come after me, because if I were a relative or a girlfriend then I should be there, in the shelter, with an ID, my picture on the authorization and everything. But what can I do? I mean, tell me! I can't even sleep at night because of that man, I came down here in the middle of the night, really, I got out of bed and came down here because I was suddenly convinced he was trying to contact me, calling me, like by telepathy, and I get here and what's he doing but sleeping! I don't know if it's me or what, you know, my imagination going wild or something, but look, just look, he's looking at me again—still, I don't think I can take much more of this."

(Click.)

"It's just our guilty consciences at work. We sort of invent things above and beyond what actually goes on inside there. Didn't you see that guy on TV, he looked pretty good, and he was in there, with all the stuff we see going on and everything. What they've done is to create some sort of collective hallucination."

(Click.)

"All I can say is I'm at peace with myself, with my conscience."

"But—your own son!"

"Look, I told him time and time again, I gave him advice, but do you think he'd listen? So what could I do? I came here, I talked with the authorities, and they came to pick him up—I asked them not to hurt him, of course—and now he's here, being rehabilitated. I'm an old man, I'm tired, I just couldn't handle him anymore. Not on my own. So I figure it like this, they're doing me a service."

(Click.)

"But it's so utterly transparent. It doesn't look like there's any glass at all."

"Are you crazy? I mean how could you explain how we act, how we see things, if there's no glass? Nothing would make any sense without the glass! We've constructed our reality, our world around that glass, you can't say it doesn't exist. Of course it exists."

(Click.)

"Look at it this way: the recent settlement at our firm is just the approach venture capitalists have been looking for, the perfect means to improve relations with the working class, in the context of the real balance of power. We entrepreneurs must continue to find ways to free ourselves from the old paternalistic laws regulating salaries and to confront the new reality, availing ourselves of the criteria of productivity. Everything is under control, absolutely under control."

(Click.)

"Just tell me. I mean I just wonder why anyone would go there practically every day."

"To watch. To watch those things."

"*Those* things?"

"You know—the things. The prisoners."

(Click.)

"Well, look who's here! I figured you'd turn up sometime."

"Hey! Long time no see. So you still come by and have a look now and then, heh?"

"Now and then. Haven't seen you for ages, though. It's like you disappeared."

"I've been real busy. You know how it is, mortgage payments to meet, the whole works. So how's life been treating you?"

"Oh, I'm getting along. Nothing much new."

"Someone you know inside?"

"No, it's just on the route. What about you?"

"Me too, just came by to have a look, that's all. The papers hardly mention the place anymore. I was wondering if anything had changed."

"I guess we all got used to the idea . . ."

"So what've you been up to? How are the kids?"

"Fine, just fine. Growing like weeds."

LOST & FOUND

"I woulde that you take this for a lesson and also, if it can be usefull to you, as the final entertaynment offerd to the person who finds himselfe absorbd in suche diffycult specullations."

(Estevam de Saa Perdigão—Commemorative of the Discoverie of Lost Golde.)

These stories, or mysteries, are all a game of words.

Whoever unravels the third mystery wins a prize: gold. The first mystery, an invention of one Martinho Dias in 1699, was solved by Estevam de Saa Perdigão in 1827; I solved mystery number two, Perdigão's consummate creation, in 1968, inheriting both the gold and the obligation; the third mystery I myself have devised.

As I recount these interweaving stories I reveal the secret and at the same time liberate myself from anxiety and responsibility. After all, I could die suddenly, and to fail to return this legacy the same way I received it, to interrupt the alternating riddle which has been going on for nearly three centuries, to break the chain which has been linked together by who knows what mysterious forces, without understanding where all this may lead, or what it links together, or how many centuries it will go on—no—no, that is something I don't dare do. I feel I have a duty. In a way these stories are too simple for so much mystery, and yet it is a complicated tale I have to tell.

A certain ritualistic procedure is unavoidable. I mean to hide my mystery in a secure place, visible yet invisible, a beautiful, transparent envelope where it will remain for years and years—perhaps a century if I do my job as well as the others—until finally some inquisitive person, exploring path after path, finds the trail and discovers the treasure at the top of the mountain. The two who came before me also used the printed word to reveal and conceal their secrets, and in one way or another hid them beneath the transparencies and reflections of glass. So.

There is nothing relating to Martinho Dias to be found in history besides a manuscript in which he recounts a crime of murder and a discovery of gold. Apparently, Dias was among those working with Borba Gato in search of gold mines, though his name only found its way into print in 1827 when a cattle driver from the back country of the river Tanque found a bottle in a grotto somewhere in the Piedade Mountains containing the following message, subsequently published in the Rio de Janeiro Gazette:

> Manuel de Borba Gato having found in the years around 1688 along the banks of the Sabará and the other great river nearby a large quantity of gold and diamonds, and being very well pleased with his find and having made his dwelling there, it happened that Fernão Dias Pais on his return from emerald discoveries in the wilderness arrived at Gato's residence in ill health and remained there, being received with hospitality by his son-in-law and fellow countryman, and in a short time died, leaving to Gato all his provisions and munitions. The following year Dom Rodrigo de Castelo Branco entered the Sabará region in the office of Superintendent of Mines and, desiring also to take advantage of the emerald discoveries, he requested from Gato a portion of the provisions left to him by Pais; and with the refusal of this request Dom Rodrigo became angry, verbally abusing Gato, whereupon I quitted him of his life without waiting for his calmer reflection, in defense of Gato's honor, he being our captain; and, fearing that the dead man's companions would return the favor, or that I would be arrested and brought to trial, with Gato's approval I withdrew from the region, with the intention of not straying too far and of prospecting for new mines, so as to report each week to the Captain any new lodes, and thus with an Indian called Inhambe as my guide I followed the mountain range which crosses the larger of the two rivers, making many passes through the range and continually finding more or less gold, until the Indian bade me go to the top

with him, to the highest peak of the aformentioned *cordillera* to a
point where one could see for a great distance, and in a notch facing
the place the Indian said was called Caeté we found a vein containing black sand with yellow bands studded with large nuggets as well
as flat scales of gold, this being a fathom and a half wide, seeded with
fine gold almost as far as the eye could see, and with no more than a
hoe we extracted eight pounds which we brought to Gato along with
the news of our great discovery, whereupon he resolved to depart
immediately for the mine but did not, as meanwhile letters from the
Governor arrived on behalf of the King granting him pardon for his
part in the death of Dom Rodrigo and naming him Lieutenant General on the condition that he point out the locations of the mines
of the Sabará, which he did willingly, indicating only those he had
personally found while keeping the grand new discovery to himself;
and seeing that he was not disposed to arrange a pardon for me for
my part in Dom Rodrigo's murder, and that he intended to conceal
this new find from everyone including the Governor, I realized that
after I had shown him the site he was planning to take my life also
and keep the glory of the new discovery for himself, and thus without
telling anyone I returned to the site in the company of my Indian
guide and with great effort and thirst, as there was no water at all to
be found, and with much difficulty, I extracted more than two stone
of gold, and with this treasure in my possession I am undertaking to
make my way to Porto Seguro from there to embark for Lisbon to ask
the King for pardon for my crime as well as for a company of armed
men to protect me from the hostilities of Gato I might encounter as
I continue in this discovery, and meanwhile not wishing to confide
my secret in anyone I inscribe here two commemorative accounts
bearing the same message, carrying one with me and leaving the
other hidden in this place, so that in the case I do not arrive at my
destination, God being better served by my death, the fortunate
person who finds this in a better time than I may enjoy the fruits of

this discovery. 12th of January, the Year of our Lord 1699. Martinho Dias.[1]

One question: why didn't everyone who read this document in the newspaper, and before them whoever found the manuscript in the first place, go out looking for the gold themselves? Perhaps they did. There are stories . . . but they are stories. You can't really believe them, these uncommemorated memories.

It is said there was a man who lived in Santa Luzia on the river das Velhas and was very mysteriously rich without planting, selling, thieving, mining, or marrying—without even friends. His only stock (as they tell it) consisted of a Tapa-cu parakeet and one slave. He liked to rock back and forth in his hammock all day and was considered a madman; sometimes he would let out great peals of laughter, rocking back and forth, back and forth. People peered in at him from the street. Once a year he would take a trip, no one knew where. But he always seemed to have gold coins to exchange, already quite a rarity in the eighteen hundreds. It was said that he had a trunkful, a whole mint hidden away in the house, a counterfeiter's die. When he was drunk and people asked him where the gold pieces came from he would say, "Tapa-cu," and point to the parakeet on his shoulder, as if to say the bird shat gold, and he'd laugh and laugh. The things people said about that guy! they said he went out at night and screwed around with the negresses on the banks of the river. They said his coins were stamped with the tail of the devil. They said he had a hidden gold mine—and that the Magistrate of Sabará was investigating the origin of his gold pieces. On his birthday a long line of unfortunates—poor, sick, blind, leprous, crippled, slaves—wound all

[1]This document (reproduced here in present-day English) appears in the bimonthly publication of the Brazilian Institute of History & Geography, Rio de Janeiro, April-May 1962, p. 85, and was republished in the Brazilian collection *Terra e Alma* (Earth and Soul), brought out by Editora do Autor in 1967, in the volume on Minas Gerais (the state of General Mines), with texts chosen by Carlos Drummond de Andrade, p. 17.

through the streets of the city to his door to receive one *mil réis* of alms; it was the only charity he gave all year and it cost him a fortune. One afternoon, when they realized his hammock hadn't been rocking back and forth for some four days, they came in and found the house turned inside out—but not one gold coin to be found. They say it was the slave who killed him and then disappeared. There's so much *buzzbuzzbuzz*ing around these mountains and mines, the *zumzum* of overworked bees who don't produce a drop of honey, just a *zumzumzum* getting History all confused: because they say this man was called Martinho Dias! There's an absurd error of more than a hundred years in this tale, or a strange coincidence of names, or some missing link which was lost from bee to bee as the name trickled down the river das Velhas rolling slowly along with its gold. It just doesn't fit together. No honey.

The true story was drowsing in the archives. Again and again I felt the gentle nagging: but what about the gold? What about the gold in this story? (Some sort of tremulous premonition? Was the man dead two hundred and some-odd years sick and tired of indifference, could he be trying to tell me something?) I questioned several pack-rats who specialize in the history of the mines. Nah, it must be one of the places up near Caeté, nah, Barão de Cocais, around there somewhere. But which one, exactly which one? No one knew. I wandered the hillsides, I scaled the summits, I slid down the slopes of Caeté: nothing. I pored over old papers, royal decrees, land grants, proclamations, lists of provisions, letters, government documents, wills—Martinho Dias's mine was nowhere to be found. (What if it had yet to be discovered?) I imagined Martinho Dias fleeing on foot to Porto Seguro with his two stone of gold. Two months of anxiety, perhaps more, depending on the January-February rains. At the edge of a river, on some mountain path, he met— what? Indians, bandits, militia, a jaguar, Borba Gato, some other ambitious man, a snake? Martinho Dias never arrived in Lisbon.

Oh, those papers . . . so eloquent you could almost picture people's faces, the cities draining of people in the race to the mines, King Dom Pedro II watching the gold slip through his fingers into alien hands all along the paths through the forest: Protect my gold! he shouted, and the governors protected it, all right, but for themselves. The troops dispersed, leaving the coast unprotected, the governor of Rio de Janeiro complained: "I finde myself more and more alone eache day, fewer soldiers and fewer inhabitants, and the exceedyng number flee-ing to the mines gives us to understande that soon there will bee no one left," even with all the commissioned officials—purveyors, magis-trates, clerks, superintendents, judges, solicitors, treasurers, smelters, minters, notaries, investigators, auditors, allocators, bailiffs, tax col-lectors, priests, militiamen—all of them incapable of containing the constant flow of people; stop the embezzlement of my gold! thundered King Dom Pedro II from Portugal—but it was impossible to control such fever, such general greed. Close the roads to and from Bahia, the Church shall send no more priests, keep close watch over all rivers and ports! the governor decreeing searches for any "soldiers founde in Minas, whereupon they shalle be chased away, and made to leeve, it not being consented that they staye there or settle in any place"; goldsmiths were banned, every necklace represents a suspicion, prostitutes arriving and draping themselves in gold; for the love of God stop the women from traveling to Minas, and "permit not that the slaves wear silkes, neither furs, nor golde, in order to thus remove from them the power to incite others to sinne with such costly ornaments in their attyres," ordered the King, and gold is hidden in hollow tree trunks, in functionaries' chests and lockers, in crevices in walls, the majority of it disappearing in the form of gold dust into the hands of foreign monarchs and the smaller part "is that whiche abydes in Portugal and the Brazilian cities: save that whiche is squanderd on chaines, hoops, and other jewelrie seen heapd upon the negresses and coloured women of the low lyfe"; so many battles, God in heaven! so many battles, betrayals in the thickets, and the martinho diases of the world finding gold for others, without tools or provisions, their adventure giving way to the venture of the Camargos, the Paes, the Pedrosos, Cardosos, Guerras, Lemos, Pires, Arzões, Gatos, Cabrals, Buenos, Furtados, while all the anonymous diases, silvas, oliveiras, scoundrels, simpletons, *pereiras, peixotos,* the rabble, the underdogs, the refuse of history, the niggers, mestizos, Indians, new-Christians, white riffraff, black riffraff, are missing from these bygone tomes of the mines, are busy hunting for gold, Indians, fugitive slaves, changing the history of Europe; and the crimes in these mines, God in heaven! the slave hunter arrives with the ears of three thousand rebellious blacks; I'd need a cavalry company, explains the Count of Assumar, in order to "establishe order and tranquilitie amoung these people; many are fugitives and killers, wandering the lengthe and breadthe of the countryside committyng many crimes"; right, quite right, agrees His Majesty Dom João, the fifth by that name, "it shall be lefte to youre discretion, my deare Count," but the important thing is that no one should channel my gold into his own pocket, the gold must continue to arrive in well-armed fleets, and do look out for those cursed pirates, will you, take care to collect all proper duties and taxes, Assumar!—take care with my royal fifth of all gold produced, my *fintas,* my *dizimas,* my *redizimas,* neither neglecting the *propinas,* the gratuities, the surcharges, the tolls, the *vinteras,* and the dowry for the Queen of England, take care of it all, you scoundrel! and the rabble goes on mining gold, adding riches to riches: take the land, men, by the acre, and gather, dig, drill, chisel, mine—but a fifth of that gold is mine, warns the King; wool, silk, ships, weapons, buttons, these are furnished to us by fair England, fraternal, chilly, industrious England, and we need to pay our English relations well, arrange a few juicy deals for them, eh, Assumar? and cattle are raised, horses tamed, comestibles planted, brandy distilled, churches gilded, houses built, ladies adorned, gentlemen dressed smartly; there's so much gold it's hard to control the exchange, which is good business for our foreign friends; but what about all the corruption, Your Majesty?—robberies and contraband and "so muche golde being taken out of the Kingdom and all its territorys in searche of better value elsewhere," the Royal Mint of Rio de Janeiro admonishes Lisbon, requesting a "curative for the verie considrable embezzlment being practisd by the businessmen of the Realme, together with the foreigners of even larger investment; thus is the golde and silver of the Realme being depleted" and the rabble keeps on digging for gold, gems, diamonds, and the Camargos, the Paes, the Pedrosos, Cardosos, Guerras, Lemos, Pires, Arzões, Gatos, Cabrals, Buenos, Futados, Franças, Nardes, Viannas go on taking possession of wilderness, rivers, trails, pastureland, all for the greater glory of His Majesty and the splendor of His court among all others, and so the King doesn't want to hear about it, screw the Solicitor General and all his lamentations, blahblah this, My Lord Dom João that, "millions and millions of foreign wares are coming into the Kingdom whiche serve onlie for luxurie and not for the necessitys of life," blahblahblah-blahblahbloo, but, Your Grace, "if these and other numerous goodes whiche serve only for luxurie were prohibited, then that much less golde woulde leave the Realme," oh what a pain, after all, don't we have that whole gang over there digging up the entire blessed earth of Brazil, mining gold and quantities of gems, planting sugar cane, fattening cattle, and don't we have all those loyal subjects over there paying their taxes, our, trusted servants doing their good work, plus all that immeasurable land still to settle and explore? But you see, my Enlightened Sovereign, blahblahblah this and that, it seems to the Royal Council that it would be best if "all goodes not manufacturd in the Realme bee prohibited, unless they come from our Indian colonys or from Macão, and the expedient course in this regarde woulde be to establish factorys within the Realme whiche produce suche products, and the extremlie necessary materials whiche foreign nations now bring us," oh what a royal pain, these people with domestic tunnel vision don't understand that we're financing a revolution in England—imagine, Mr. Solicitor, a revolution which is creating a new system of production in which machines will work more and men less; and afterward we shall

take advantage of their learning and with our gold will be able to make
more and better, and so put that rabble to work, Count Governor! So
the martinho diases, the ragamuffins, the riffraff and underdogs pan for
gold in tired gravel beds, and to the wealthy owners of property and
slaves go the large, productive mines—Lisbon urgently needs that gold,
fellows!—some of the blacks are allowed to prospect on their own as
long as they pay to their masters so much per day, they can even sell
brandy and tasty tidbits: instead of taking gold out of the mountain,
they take gold from the people who've been to the mountain, so much
the difference; some of them even wear fine fabrics, a handkerchief
tucked at the sleeve, a weapon at the belt!—but look how bold these
Negroes are getting, we must warn the proper whites, only the proper
ones, for the ragamuffin whites are already out liberating black women
and marrying them, there just are not enough white women to go
around, long live the brown race of Brazil; the suffering on that mountain, God in heaven! the place for insubordinate Negroes is in the pillory, Lisbon applauds, Revolt! the order comes down to shoot the leaders,
"carrying out the execution if possyble in locations moste useful for
terror and example," forced labor for the followers, flogging for the
troublesome, and "they shoulde only bee permitted to bee clothd in the
simplest sackcloth and only as muche as necessarie to cover their na-
kedness and shielde them from the inclemencie of the weather, so that
thus they will lose their pryde and come to see that they were borne to
be the white man's slaves"; not even free blacks or mulattoes may wear
fine clothing, the pillory for any who insist; Assumar, Assurnar, clamors
the King, "I have beene informd that many mills have beene constructed
for the distillation of firewater," yes, it's true, Sire, God Save You, and I
shall take appropriate action since the proliferation of liquor in Minas is
already causing irreparable damage to "your royale goodes as well as to
the tranquilitie of the local inhabitants, due to disturbances caused by
drunken negroes, also depryving us of their service in the mines themselves"; well then, be vigilant, my dear Pedro d'Almeida, establish order

in the North with corrals and in the South with grain fields and the best shall always fall to the most loyal, and to the others less; Do this, Assumar, my good, zealous friend, and hang who you must!

In the midst of this heap of papers I discovered—but wait, I'm a bit uncomfortable with the first person. Instead I think I'll refer to myself as the Author: it's more modest, more appropriate.

Well then. Among archival items such as "The Martyrios Estate," the Author found a letter which was disturbing, in spite—or because—of the presence of a certain self-martyring religious fanaticism:

Second of February:
From this yeare of our Lorde one thousand eight hundred and thirty-three, I sende to you my most cordiall salutations along with the inlightenment needed to attaine the felicitie wich has been giv'n to me, herewith the following:
You must assend the mountain called Itapucu with the crosse of the Miracle, place there sayd crosse, driving into the extremitys the Foure Nailes of the Martyr, and speccullate on the Mistery. Excepting that this reflexion must be accomplished at first light or the Grace will be denied you; further, it being to all advantage to perform suche with discression in order that these joyfull reserves shall have no ende nor exaction.
Estevam de Saa Perdigão.

Immediate perturbations in the Author's mind: where and what was the place called Itapucu? Wasn't an exaction some kind of tax or something like that? What if the mine really were yet to be discovered? And what could the purpose of the letter be—a letter addressed to no one, addressed to the future: The Author recopied the letter with premonitory goosebumps.

He commenced an investigation in the Public Archives of Minas. Just who was this Estevarn de Saa Perdigão? The last owner of the considerable estate called Martírios, located on the Piracicaba River. Time frame? The records found at the estate indicate that Perdigão died, an old man, in 1835. What did the property produce? Sugar, cane liquor, cattle. How did he acquire it? Inherited from his father, probably Manuel de Saa Perdigão. Any children? None that the records attest to. Siblings? Twelve are documented, but nothing is known of them. Who, then, inherited Martírios? His Highness, Regent Dom Pedro II, who subsequently named an administrator. And when did Perdigão's father purchase the property? Unknown. Who was he? Unknown. Records exist of a Manuel Perdigão who abandoned the military life for the spiritual in 1706, but it is impossible to confirm that it was he. Where is this mountain located? Currently no mountain by the name Itapucu is known in the immediate area of the estate, nor in the area of the river Piracicaba, nor the river Tanque, nor das Velhas nor Doce. What does Itapucu mean? In the Tupi Indian language it means long or tall rock. Does it appear in other documents? Yes—the name Itapucu, spelled Itapucu, appears in two 1701 land grants ceding property to Borba Gato!

And so the Author traveled south from Itabira, searching for a mountain with a name that sounded like Itapucu, with a "long stone," on the ancient lands of Borba Gato.

Sorry, sir, not around here. Never heard of it.

A short time after Martinho Dias's disappearance General Borba Gato petitioned for ownership of these lands. Very suspicious.

Not as far as I know, mister, not unless it's over in the Piedade range, there's all kinds of hills over there.

Martinho Dias had not revealed to Borba Gato the location of the strike. Could the general just have gone looking for it at random between the Paraopeba and Piracicaba rivers?

Not here, no. Nothing like that. Maybe you should look over in the Itatiaia Mountains . . .

Impossible. Gato must have had some idea of the route at least, and he applied for the whole parcel—not just because it probably would include the site of Martinho Dias's gold mine, but also because the land was valuable.

I've never heard of a name like that here in Nova Era.

There was no apparent link between the letters of Perdigão and Dias, except for a keen sense of disquiet in the Author's mind.

No, I don't know that mountain, or any estate named Martírios, for that matter. If it was around here it's been defunct a long time.

And another disturbing fact: both Dias and Perdigão, one hundred thirty-four years apart, addressed their letters to chance, left them for the benefit and use of the person who was to find them, whoever and whenever that might be.

A long time ago I remember some place around here that was called Mount Agudo—that's sort of like what you're looking for, isn't it? The British mining company demolished it completely, though: it was leveled to the ground.

One letter bequeathed material riches, the other promised spiritual gains. But . . .

Well, it sounds familiar, but I'm not sure . . . There's long, tall rocks with Indian names all over the place, you know? Up there, Piedade, Caraça, there's a long rock. And off that way, in the Curral range, stretching down there, there's a place called long rock. Any mountain that looks to be made of rock they call long rock. But I don't know any by the name Itapucu, that I never heard of. I've got a pal, though, who knows this country better than the birds.

Two words stood out in Perdigão's almost incoherent letter, words borrowed from the world of gold and slipped in among all those others from the world of religion: reserves and exaction—capital and tax. There they sat—incognito, exasperating, like someone who gives with one hand and takes away with the other.

Heh-heh, heh-heh-heh, who told you all that nonsense, heh-heh-heh, heh-heh-heh, hmmm? Look friend, I know the place you're talking about, heh-heh, it's not called that anymore, used to be. When we were kids running around these hills hunting birds and little stone beads, in those days there was a hill folks used to call Tapacu, heh-heh, but nobody called it Tapacu, heh-heh-heh, it was called Big Hill, there was even a mine there, the Big Hill Mine.

In a flash the Author saw it all: the man with the gold coins in Santa Luzia, tapa-cu was what he used to say, it was Itapucu in Perdigão's message, Tapacu to old man heh-heh-heh, Ita-pucu to Borba Gato—all the same thing, variations of the same word, and Martinho Dias's gold had already been exposed, exploited, exhausted. He would climb Big Hill to examine the scars of the mine, no longer the feverish frontiersman but an archival rat confirming his instincts; on the basis of the fleeting facts in his possession he would go there, unriddle the two-hundred-eighty-year-old secret, locate that peak lost in the historical documents which miners had apparently found by chance, and discover a wooden sign nailed into the rock with four large iron spikes which formed a diamond shape bearing the inscription:

"Site of the discoverie of muche golde in the yeare 1699; God will make it to shine when He is servd."

The scars at the base of the mountain, the mouth of the mine closed for more than a century, the sign there at the top—they told the whole story. He descended Big Hill with only a tale to tell.

And he was just beginning to tell it when he thought—no! there's something to this after all. Traditionally there were only three Nails of the Martyr—why did Perdigão's letter mention four? A vision: Perdigão's smiling, mocking face.

Of course, of course—explains the history professor. And not just in terms of Brazilian tradition. In the Middle Ages the crucifixion was depicted with four nails, two for the feet and two for the hands. But by the close of the Middle Ages and the beginning of the Renaissance, the crucified Lord had come to be represented with one single nail through his feet, one foot crossed over the other. Which is the tradition in Brazilian crucifixes. Exactly.

It's a matter of repertoire—pronounces the professor of Communication Theory. Consider the three signs: Miracle, Martyr, Mystery—two seven-letter, three-syllable words with initial stress and between them one six-letter, two-syllable word with initial stress, all beginning with an iconic/rhematic Qualisign—forgive me, the letter M. Coincidence? Impossible: there is no such thing as chance in a text. Any text is the result of a repertoire, on conscious and unconscious levels, and can only be decoded by someone privy to the same repertoire. Miracle is a Rheme—forgive me, a First, for which we need to approach an interpretation, or a Second, in order to incorporate it in a correlation,—or a Third. Miracle, Martyr, Mystery, these three signs are most probably indicators meant to call the reader's attention to certain objects, objects which perhaps no longer exist, which were lost in time. Or else we just don't possess the semantic repertoire to be able to recognize them.

Yes, there's something to that. Objects which perhaps no longer exist, like Itapucu—or do exist, but with another name. Lost references. Words inside words. Built-in signs. Alliteration, anagrams, paranomasias—is that where the secret of the text is to be found? The Author searched for clues in the voco-visual relationship between Miracle, Martyr, and Mystery, dividing the letters, studying their relation to the text as a whole as well as to each other—which, on the basis of Latin roots, he took to mean "mirar mare mistierium": one must look to the sea. But there was no sea in Minas, so this would have to be interpreted as searching, prospecting for gold in the Sierra do Mar Mountains. Or, if it were "mira/marte/mister," marte = Mars, that hypothesis would take him to the ridge which seen from Itapucu was located directly under the planet Mars. And so on. He spent hours and hours cross-breeding words and coming up with all sorts of hybrids, but nothing led him to the gold. At each try he could see the ghostly Perdigão, wearing the superior smile of someone who proposes a game and follows his adversary's progress—hot, then cold—but without supplying any help, poker-faced.

But what if this diabolical Perdigão, instead of calling attention to particular objects, was intentionally trying to throw him off course? Perhaps the words had other meanings? Lost references—no—hidden references. Metaphors. He began searching for clues in the sense of the words. And there was Perdigio's smile: simultaneously hoping his adversary would be unable to discover the trick, proof of the ingenuity of his creation, and yet inwardly wishing for him to discover it and testify to its inventiveness: gee whiz, that was a real bull's-eye, you're something else, Perdigão, congratulations, right on the money. Son-of-a-bitch!

After working over the passages of secondary importance, he isolated what seemed to him the pivotal sentence: "You must assend the mountain called Itapucu with the Crosse of the Miracle, place there sayd crosse, driving into the extremitys the Foure Nailes of the Martyr, and specullate on the Mistery." "Miracle" was the most intriguing word here. He did some checking: derived from the Latin *miraculu*. The Cross of the Miracle. The cross of Christ—four nails, four letters? Christ, Cristo, Cryst, Chryspto—yes, "Xpto," the medieval abbreviation for Christ, from the Greek: XPTO, X for Christ (and X—the cross—marks the spot), P for Passion, T for *tellus*, earth (and what is under the earth!), O for—what?—oh, hell, this is going nowhere. Perdigão smiling again. Back to "Miracle." Same word origin as *miracle* in French, same meaning. And *miraculu* comes from *mirari*, to look, to admire . . . the cross of looking, admiring, mire, mirage, mirador. Does this make any sense? Perdigão smiles. (Is it just the Author's imagination or is Perdigão's smile fading?) *Mirari*, mirador, mirage, always the idea of looking. The Cross of the Mirador—a place from which to look, to look for gold, a mirage. Perdigão was smiling again. The Author pursued the root in French, in English, came up with *miroir*—that's it: mirror! The Cross of the Mirror, a Mirror Cross. Reflection! First light!

—Ah, Perdigão, you son-of-a-bitch, now I've got you!

Suddenly it was simple, and in his enthusiasm he shouted and pointed at the pale ghost: I take the Mirror Cross, fix it in place of the sign you installed at the top of the hill, fasten it down inserting the four nails in the four holes forming the shape of a diamond, and speculate—ah, the poetic son-of-a-bitch—speculate, a verb meaning to ponder, investigate, and also it's the light of the mirror—a looking glass or speculum—speculate on the Mystery, meaning the gold, and this investigation with the light/reflection of the mirror, yes, and this reflection, meaning light *and* thought, meditation, this reflection, as he says, must be accomplished, performed, at the first light of day; that way the Grace can be attained—meaning the gold—but it must be kept secret so these reserves will have no end—how could they end if they're so vast? Or does he mean so they won't end up in alien hands, is that it? And also to avoid paying taxes, "no end nor exaction" (just between us, pretty lousy alliteration). Signed, the old bastard tax evader himself, Estevam de Saa Perdigão.

And so the Author climbed Big Hill once more (was it just his imagination or had the dimming ghost's mouth twisted into a smile just before he disappeared?) to measure the distance between nail holes and figure the precise length and width of the Mirror Cross. "God will make it to shine when He is served"—Perdigão's exasperating sense of humor.

One cold July night he set out tugging a mule behind him on which he had tied the mirror-glass cross, protected between two crosses made of thin wood. It's a Promise, he explained to the curious. So now even mules are making promises? he heard his pal heh-heh-heh mumble, and the Author walked off without bothering to answer, heh-heh-heh. He set up the cross and prayed for light. The first day was no good—cloudy and cold; but the second dawned bright and clear. The light was reflected out onto the shadows of an almost inaccessible notch in the opposite ridge, about three kilometers away. He studied the spot, noting carefully trees, rocks, the profile of the hill, and walked straight there armed with pickax, sleeping bag, food, anxiety. Nothing. He found nothing.

He stayed overnight, in fear of snakes, dreaming of that last smile of Perdigão's. The third morning the sun reflected from the larger Mirror Cross on the hill opposite confirmed that he was in the right place. He found nothing. Sat down perplexed and ran through Perdigão's letter again, lingering over each word, humbled once more by the cunning of that man one hundred-fifty years distant. He could find no error and yet he knew he was wrong. Damn Perdigão. Leaving everything exactly as it was when he had arrived, he hid the cross and started down the hill. It was useless to continue; he would rest his weary mind. For, as obsessed as he was, Perdigão clearly had the advantage.

Months later, he picked up the letter again. Of course: the "second of February"—not the date of the letter, but the day when the dawning light should be projected onto the mirror! The sun's and earth's positions change according to the season, and that son-of-a-bitch even took astronomy into consideration!

On the second of February, 1968, the Author calmly climbed to the summit of Itapucu, installed the cross, and saw that this time the reflection shone on a notch which was much closer, perhaps only a kilometer away. Gold? Of course there was gold. And is. Sheets of gold almost a palm across, gold nuggets thicker than a finger. I even found—I can go back to the first person now, at last—one nugget that weighed about six hundred grams, almost pure gold.

So that's the story. And the legacy that whoever unravels my mystery will inherit.

Digging deeper below the notch in the ridge I find, buried, a wooden box coverd with copper. Humidity has seeped into the nail holes, rusting the metal and rotting the wood, but the pages of a fat book, the kind you would picture a scribe bending over, are still intact. Under the soft cover lie one hundred sheets of thick paper, pages and pages of grand flourishes—handwriting, so difficult to read, of long ago. I read:

COMMEMORATIVE
by
Estevarn de Saa Perdigão
of
The Discoverie
of
LOST GOLDE
preceeded by the unsuccessfull dilligences of
his Father
MANUEL DE SAA PERDIGÃO
This Yeare of our Lorde MDCCCXXXIII

All the misadventures of the Perdigãos were borne of venture. Arriving in his twentieth yeare in the region of the Mines, or Minas, as this captaincy was then calld, the honorable sargeant my Father was enstructed to guarde with dilligents *diligence* the passages to Bahia and Porto Seguro in order to prevent the purloyning of golde dust, in which he did indeed demonstrate muche severitie, searching the trunks and bundles of those travellers who were coming and going, trading in cattel *cattle* and other goodes of Bahia, his zeale being muche appreciated and esteemd by the Goverror, Dom Antonio de Albuquerque.

Straying from the root *route* one day, entertaind to give chase to a birde which seduced his eares and eyes, he encounterd in the middle of the forrest two skeltans, one of whom was a gentleman and the other a heathan *an Indian and a white—it's Martinho Dias!* and as theyr haire and clothing and weppons *weapons* were remarkablie in order my Father understoode that they surely had died from the byte of a poisonous animal or from fevere. His were the furst *first* human eyes to have gazed upon these bones, for all they had possessed was present and intact save their lives; at their feet were fownde *what? oh—were found* two bundles

which my Father opend in feare of poisonous spiders and scorpians
which had killd so many and were still killing all over Minas, and the
two bundles opend reveald sufficient golde to weigh two stone. He was
exceedingly carefull not to produce any forme of commoxion to attract
the people going by on the path beside the river belowe. Allong with the
riches there was a letter *the other copy!* which told of the murder of the
nobleman Dom Rodrigo de Castelo Branco by the author of sayd letter
and giving seerninglie valuble indications regardyng the whereabouts
of the secret mines from which this golde had come *seeminglie valuble ha
ha I can already see this guy searching all over for that fool mine and finding
exactly nothing because that damn letter leads exactly nowhere, I'd just like
to know how these Perdigãos finally got their hands on that gold following*
seeminglie valuable indications regardyng the whereabouts of the secret
mines from which this golde had come, in the forme and manner copyd
here from those originall instructions.

"Manuel de Borba Gato having founde in the yeares around 1688
allong the banks of the Sabarâ and the other great rivere nearby a
large quantitie of golde and diamonds *I know this letter only too well*
Dom Rodrigo enterd the Sabarâ *etc.* and requested a portion of the
provisions *babababababa, no need to read it, babababa* with an Indian
calld Inhambe as my *same old thing* more than two stone of golde *etc.
etc. and then the ending:* in a better time than I may enjoie the fruits
of this discoverie. 12th of January 1699. Martinho Dias."

Considering himselfe blessed by fortune my Father hid his finde well
for another occasion so as to collect it without dispute and did commence to serche for the myne with the intention of reaping somethyng
something from it before another shood finde it by chance, and without
reportyng the finde to the Superintendent of Mines, at that tyme the
same Borba Gato, all this in goode conscience since it seemd to him
most reasonable to in this way give prejudice to the Kinge instead of

letting the Superintendent give prejudice to bothe of them, himselfe and the Kinge, for being poore himselfe he could filch lesse from the Kinge than the other, thus in fact addyng to the Royale Treasurie rather than dimynishyng it. Everyone contravend the Lawe *broke the law* in this particular, at riske of not receiving lande rights in rewarde for the discoverie they had made, since what would be givn'n them accordyng to the Regime would be giv'n to whoever denouncd them for hidden golde: in this waye everyone proseeded to hide a quantitie of golde before reporting theyr finde. *And it wasn't even a sin, since the priests themselves had established the difference between civil obligations and obligations of conscience—they had their own interests to look after, the scoundrels! In confessional after confessional the faithful learned that taxes were a civil duty but that shirking this duty didn't mean going to hell. The only ones who paid were the ones on the King's side or anyone afraid of being fingered.*

My Father attempted the extremely difficult indeavor to locate those veynes of golde in the rugged wildernesse for months, and hard months they were, but Martinho Dias's enstructions were not sufficient to finde anythyng. This came to passe around the tyme of the death of King Dom Pedro II, *let's see, that makes it . . . damn, I thought I had all this stuff down, after all the time I spent in those archives—must be 1707, yes* resultyng in the perpetuall disillusionment in which the Perdigãos lived. The sadnesse of possessing the golde and not possessing it, changing them into persons who could not beare to admire the remarkable thyngs God endowd to Nature or to assend a hill or peake without the expectation of there being golde in't.

I pray your pardon for my antiquated stile and beg that you not en-tertayne a lower estimation of this Commemorative on account of the errors, for the actions herein are deservyng of a reader tho' the writing be not; and the writing is thus for the reason of there being no teacher of reading and writing in the wildernesse of Martyrios, nor of Gram-mar nor Rhetoric, since the village of Nossa Senhora da Conceição das Minas Novas de Antonio Dias would paye no litterie *literary* subsidie:

thus it was my father who enstructed *instructed* me in reading, writing and arythmetic. What books there were in Martyrios were the Religious Narratives which contaynd *contained* the lives of the saints, the serche for the Holy Graile, recounting the memorable storie of the Knights of the Rounde Table of Camelot, and the Loyale Counsellor, from whose pages could be learnt practicall teachings and Proverbs. Books there were also by one Perdigão who wayted upon the Governor of Minas in his letters, records, and provisions, and these were storys of the pilgrimmages of the travellers through the Conquests of the Realme. Hence I write this commemorative in the best waye I can, following what I understande of the Loyale Counsellor who teaches: write things of goode substance clearlie, in order to be well understood, and as elegantlie as possible, and consise when it be necessarie, and in this indeavor make use of paragraphs and punctuate wisely.

Seeing that he could not hope to discover that riche veyne working only on Sundays and Holie Days, my Father left his poste as sergeant, allong with its exemptions and privilleges, and bought the lande lying closest to the Carmo and Caetê mines, where came to be erected the splendid Estate of Martyrios. While the great house was being constructd *constructed* by the finest artisans of Villa Rica he proceeded with his envestigation of that extensive wildernesse, ever tormented with the belyfe that he was standing on top of the golde and yet could not discerne it; which is why he enstructd himselfe in the practise of the examination of the qualitie of golde, becomyng an expert knowne for his infallibilitie.

With the reste of his reserves he purchasd twelve slaves to worke the fields and the mynes *it's confusing this y instead of an i, there's no system to it, they all seem to change it around whenever it suits them* for a very burdensome price, this being the consequence of the Royale prohibition against throngs of negroes coming to Minas (the Royale Council warned of the danger of there already being in Minas ten negroes for everie white, reasonyng that to increase this number would bee to make possible the losse

of the very mines, since already in this quantitie some negroes had arrivd
who were provoking manie disturbances, and advizing meanwhile that,
as a curative, complet severitie ought be demonstrated towards whatsoever revolts of sayd negroes, from floggyng at the foot of the pillorie, to
the most severe, that is, hangyng and quarteryng in the towne square,
for terror and example, as and accordyng to theyr sentences declard),
and my Father purchasd also beastes of burden, and some cattel, leaving
no remaynyng reserves save this dailie provender *that's a pretty word,
provender.*

The letter and the news of the golde were maintayned in supreme
secrecie by my Father, who withdrewe to Martyrios from Caetê and
livd there secluded from important people, eache day increasyngly more
afflicted by the syte of those leagues of fields unpeopled by cattel or other
creatures, that riche farmlande lying fallow, the neglectd clumps of trees
and patches of quince, jambo, guariroba, jabuticaba, so usefull in the
attributes of its barke in the preparation of medication for the intestynes,
jatobaas which I lyke so well mixed with honie, as well as ariticuns and
other wilde fruits; my Father not being free to tender to these *care for
them* as all his tyme was engaged in that battel of honore against the
spitefullnesse of Martinho Dias, as surely it might be calld. *That's it, that's
exactly the sensation I had—the duel against the clever snares of the text,
the pleasure of deciphering, the fascination of the game and the mystery, the
bullheadedness of Perdigão, the anger, hate, indignation, impotence! So, you
son-of-a-bitch, that's what you want, is it? To rekindle just those same, precise
feelings—a little revenge, is that it?*

My Father livd for many yeares in this drudgerie without respit,
making no improvements on the Estate, serching for the golde on
journeys which lasted monthes or weeks, trusting in Indians of various
nations who enummerated and led him to different sites called Ita-pucu,
but none of these dilligences yeelded a thyng because the peakes and
mountains and ranges and caetês are infinyte and the heathans ignorant
of metals. The people in the region did not take my Father for crazie only

because everyone in Minas Geraes busied themselves prospectyng, but he returnd lesse capacious eache time. He did finde small lodes wich he crackd open, minyng some lesser amount of golde before sending worde to the Superintendent to allot suche lode to anyone dispozed to worke it, this being hardlie worthwhile for him to dig those veins and thus employ the major force of his slaves, some of wich he had ceded for money, others tylld the fields of Martyrios and one or two negresses he kept for the kitchen and the necessetys of the bodie. These bore him children which he solde, as was then the rule. *Absurd!*

And as his tyme was filld with this struggle, he was detaynd longer in Martyrios, tired of adventure, longyng for a wife and children, which he had none of, there being few maidens in the townes and none in the hinterlandes.

It was during this tyme that a judishall *judicial* inqueste was begun regardyng a death which occurred in the golde mynes of Carmo, resulting in sayd judishall inquirie because the Roiz Saa familie had sufferd a serious offence agaynst their estate *he means pocketbook* at the hands of a neighbore, the Roiz Saa familie shooting sayd neighbor with rifle and pistols and killyng him with well-aymed leade bullets. They were thus fleeing with theyr possessions to Porto Seguro and took lodgyng at Martyrios as one of the daughters of six yeares was ill and the mother was suffring feveres and chills, both being thus presently incapable of further travell. They reveald no offence on arriving at Martyrios, taking care lest the shelter and sustenance they needed shood be denied them if the murder they committd were to become knowne.

Two days having passd they became fearfull that the arme of Justyce shood reache them, and with the urgencie of leaving and yet being unable to bring the women with them due to theyr unhealthie conditions, they apprized my Father of theyr circumstances and all the detayls of the case *uh-oh, this could go on forever—let's get back to the gold, for Christ's sake!* saying that an malevolent neighbor having encroachd four arms-lengths into the Roiz Saa myne, having enterd and mined

with resultyng great losse to theyr estate, and theyr complaynts; to the
Inspector Generall and the Superintendent of Mines being to no availe,
it seemyng to the Roiz Saas that they were all in on the plot to take the
richest mine of the familie and in this waye trick even the Governor, the
Count of Assumar, who the while simply calld for a judishall inquirie,
whyle similar invasions had beene resolvd with the precise demarcation
of lande and the obligation of the invader to pay reparations for the losse
of the other's propertys, putting an ende to continued damage. Embol-
dend by this delaye in offishall scrutinie *ha* the neighbors advanced
further into sayd myne, encounteryng opposition from the Roiz Saas,
and commencd shooting, one of the sonnes being thus wounded. The
Roiz Saas became empassiond and quit of his lyfe with many rifle and
pistoll shots the most insolente and theyr leader, then fleeing with all
theyr reserves, intendyng to make for Porto Seguro and from there to
Lisbon to enter a denunciation if it be God's will to premit *permit* theyr
arrival. The wife and daughter they left in Martyrios, wich provd to be
the ende of their martyrdom instead of yet anothere, the girl fynding a
home there and the woman dying of fevere, not longe after.

My Father attended to the little sicke childe for forty days and forty
nights, with tee *ha ha tea with two e's* and broth and plasters and scaldyng
towells, captivated by her beautie and delicacie; he sente in everie direction for a Phlebotomist who would be able to cure her with bloodletting
and purges, not fynding one due to the great lacke in those parts, but with
God's helpe she overcame her illnesse, and he lead *led* her to convalessence
through the effects of the best care with soups, legumes, and marrow. The
girle was an anjell *angel* who freed him from his avariss *avarice* for golde
through the obligation of a promise he had made praying for her salvation,
and he opend his spirit to the understandyng of higher truths, to remorse
for evile ways and to the love for all Creation.

Thus farre the tale I tell is only a storie told me though I tell it againe
and againe as my Father tolde it to me. He continued in his love of the
girl and having no worde of her relatives for the two yeares since they

departd and not desyring to leave her in any house at the discretion of
the Jurisdiction of Orphans and likewise being unable to keepe her as
a guest at Martyrios with no wyfe there abiding and not desyring that
she marrie another when grone *grown!* he decided to make her his
wyfe, with the consent of the Viker *who the hell is that?* of Caetê and
areas southe as long as he promised not to take her to wyfe before she
was fifteen yeares of age *oh, the priest.* The newes of these yeares as
she grew in yeares and beautie, learning the ways of the house and the
man, I cared not to knowe of, suche being subjects touchyng upon the
personal. *What? Is he kidding? What I'd give for a story like that—detailing
the child-bride's every moment, the husband watching her bud and having
to contain his passion, all the psychological intrigue, those long nights after
she's developed but hasn't quite reached the promised fifteen, his relief in
the dark of the night in the slave quarters, the glutton priest's watchful eye,
interpreting every gesture during his frequent visits, the innocent (or not?) girl
faced with so many ambiguous situations, the father-husband applying a little
discipline—a couple good swats on the behind—all the delicate moments
like when she goes to the city to buy a new dress, or her bewilderment
at menstruation: who should she turn to to find out what's happening to
her—her husband or the slave woman he sleeps with? And would she even
know what husband means? What would she call him—sir? Uncle Manuel?
Manny? And when the time comes for intimacies, how to signal the change
in behavior all of a sudden . . . Listen, sweetie, from now on you're my wife,
okay? No way. Unless I made the father a real brute, which was apparently
pretty common in those days. Ah, but not the girl, his mother, I'd keep her
sweet and delicate, and the father would be kind of rough-hewn but good-
hearted, I mean, after all, didn't he nurse the poor sick child back to health?
Shit, what a story! And here I am worrying about mirror-games and all kinds
of other breakable fables!*

    And suche is the storie of my Mother, Ignez Maria Carolina de Saa,
who is now with God, and all her children, my brothers, of which I am
the twelfth and last-borne, and perhaps the only one living. I was bourne

one or two yeares after the deathe of His Majestie the Kinge Dom Ioão *I guess that's João* the Fifth, in the first or second yeare of the Reigne of Dom Ioseph *José,* when my Father was in his sixty-fifth or sixty-sixth yeare; thus am I in perhaps the eightieth yeare of my age, but not so old that I feel my tyme has come; and of the yeares lacking I feele not theyr lack, and they seem to be plentious enough for I still boost *boast* a firm bodie and the firnmesse of a man in the morning. *The braggart. Probably just a piss hard-on.*

Thereupon, forgive me, thereafter, Martyrios became a reale farme, with my Father and Mother and then the children assistyng in all the worke, with prosperouss plantations of frutes for confexions, herdes of cattel for fresh and salted meates, and cane to be solde to the sugar mills; eighteen were the slaves we ownd, divyded by my Father betweene fields, stables, kitchen, and two wich were emploied prospectyng golde, an easie occupation wich would have been givn'n up entirelie if they did not produce halfe an oitava per day, and in the case that they producd more they earnd more accordinglie.

Likewise in farming my Father preferrd to applie to his negroes rewardes rather than punishments, the wich he only applied and with difficultie in cases of great lacke of respect, and those workers who producd more than an agreed upon quantitie were payd as rewarde one vintern eache day, and hence the more pleasant and productive they became. The kitchen negresses, when not occupyd with theyr pots of marmelade and other famous concoctions wich were exported by mule to Rio de Janeyro, gave themselves to the courtesys of the eight men of the hous, wich is how many we numberd, and earnd one vintem eache for the goode they accorded us *in-house prostitution!* tho' I will not relate the particulars *oh phooey* of theyr services *get this* for feare of offendyng your modestie, but bee it knowne *dirty old men, taking advantage of the setup of slavery like that—and paying them yet, to ease their consciences no doubt* bee it knowne that these actions were accomplishd with theyr pleasant approvall. *As if they had a choice.* My Father was one of the two or three slaveowners whose slaves made backe theyr purchass price in two yeares, whereas in the region of Minas it commonlie took foure or five yeares, and in this he was different from all others, behaving with gentlenesse and recompence, by the inspiration of Dona Ignez, my Mother.

My Father was a verie singulare man in the societie of men, a man of integritie and wisdom. Permit me, Sirs, to fatten this texte with the followyng account, that will not displease you. *Don't be too sure.* I accompanied him oncet to Sabarâ-bussu to joyn our mules to a caravan on its waye to Rio de Janeyro carrying the locall goodes to be solde there. It happend that my Father was surrownded by some slaveowners who did not approve the custom of rewardes establishd at Martyrios, who sayd that it would insite *incite* a revolt of the reste of the slaves in the Republic, at wich my Father defendyng himselfe argu'd with them, questioning their owne imperfections: saying it was not Christian to hire out theyr negroes, not working in field or myne themselves, this constituting usurie as they in dishonest idlenesse increasd their reserves with the worke of another, as if the slaves were money to earne interest and not, as is the fact, durable goodes, to be used in the manufacture or procurement of comestible or minerall goodes. The men did not fynd themselves in agreement with him, replying in scorne that even the religious orders rented theyr negroes and possessed reserves renderyng interest; how then could a Perdigão put himselfe to debate the Christianitie of a clerick? And he answerd that he did not thynke it much Christian of friars or clericks to have made Christians of the Indians, as they were presentlie convertyng the negroes, in order that they sould serve better and be come accustomed to strikt obedience. No doubt this was too loftie a subject for the intellect of those men, and thus he explaynd: the friars could not without lying dissuade theyr servants from theyr pagan belyfs, because it was onlie from idolatrous heathans that a Christian could appropriate propertie and subjugate without offendyng God, a Christian not being permitted to subjugate another Christian. *What a character! Fighting for ethics in slavery—a cool place in hell! From what he says, it sounds like the Indians had already been emancipated, which means if I remember correctly that this conversation must have taken place during the height of the Marquez de Pombal's power play against the Jesuits, or shortly afterward. At which point the church's morals were at an all-time low. I mean you could say things like this right in the main square—wonder if this scene was taking place in the main square? Come to think of it, this story really isn't very well told—things of no interest are prolonged and the parts which should be more fully explained are abbreviated. For instance, why did the old man use such a hidden form of payment, all those little bonuses? What did he think of work paid by-the-hour or by-the-job? The larger mills only had slaves employed in the simplest of work, back-breaking but simple. Anything dangerous—risky, potentially crippling work, where you could lose a finger or an arm or be killed—was done by salaried workers, because that way there would be no loss to the slaveowner in case of accident. Think what it would mean to cripple or maim a slave—it amounted to diminishing the owner's estate! So slaves and paid workers labored together, side by side; it was just that the owner had more regard for his slaves! And thus The only difference nowadays is there's no more slavery thus* my Father was tak'n for a liberall publickly and for a foole privately, for he wasted his vintems on something the whip could take care of at muche lesse expence, to wich charge he boldly responded: of course the whip is muche more to your tayste; and he reproved them for other crimes and offences agaynst our Lorde, for they adornd theyr most shapelie and appealyng negresses in silke dresses and golde chaynes and sent them into the streets to live a dissolute and scandalous lyfe, punishing those who did not yeeld two hundred mil réis per day *well well well, the oldest profession—and her buddy, pimping* and those most wantyn ones yeelded better than two hundred mil réis and savd the same with the intension of buying theyr freedom, but often after buying theyr freedom they caused an even greater scandall, by then being muche accustomed, indeed taking pleasure, in the lyfe of pleasure. There were already present in the square *so it is in the square!* various whytes and negroes listening who had beene captivated by the eloquents *eloquence* of that robust olde man with the long whyte bearde, some of whom seemed familliar to me, and my Father spoke to them in firme voice with the authoritie and wisdom of his eighty yeares, cautionyng one and all agaynst the usurers of slaves and of money, who would sease *seize* their farmes and mills and mynes thereby to add to theyr already extensive holdyngs, and thus would be come the only proprietors while the reste were reducd to being theyr servants, and they would be so great and powerfull that they would not onlie oppresse the poor but would create disturbances and raise insurrexions agaynst the government. *Right on the nose!* The voice of my Father was a trumpet thundring o'er the mountains, turnyng the hills upsyde downe, as he spoke also of the mistreatment customarilie practised upon slaves, above all the darkest of them and the mullatos, freed or not, and of how the masters and foremen had degraded theyr soules in the exersize of suche evile wayes; thereupon he raysed the spectre of theyr condemned futures were they to fail to correct this iniquitie, saying: the day shall come when the negroes shalle be free, as it was with the Indians, and shalle lose theyr monetarie value which, from yore point of view is all they have, and the day shalle come when whyte men corruptd by simylar eviles will take pleasure in shootyng theyr muskets and rifles killyng them as in a great hunte. *The man's a prophet.* And the people listend to him as to a profet of the Scriptures. *You bet.*

Sensing that God would soon calle him, my Father summond the whole familie to give his enstructions, thus the occasion on wich he reveald the secret of the golde *finally we get back to the gold* wich has so derangd us all; neverthelesse the discoverie was lefte to me and onlie to me, for being the person most experiencd in that matter and possessyng the most abel mind, and thus past into my handes the letter of one Martinho Dias, the invaluble defender of the infamous Borba Gato in the deathe of a nobleman; my Father sayd I was to serche for the golde onlie after his deathe, owing to a promise he had made; and finallie he sayd that I shood looke after the wellbeing of all the Perdigãos, that we shood live neither too confident of the golde we as yet not possess, nor desparing of the hope of possessing suche golde. A few monthes hence he gave up his spirit and left us.

And Dom Ioseph too past away and Dona Maria assended the throne to the great gladdnesse of the people of Minas who fownd the noveltie of the Dominion of a woman exceedinglie pleasing.

I serched without respit for the precious treasure promised in Martinho Dias's letter, as shorte on successe as I was on reste, but this narrative merits more than suche a weak prosodist as I can supplie; it requires a poet more learned, suche as the unfortunate fellow Claudio Manuel da Costa of Villa Rica whose verses upon the arduous conquest of Minas I oncet had the pleasure of hearyng; or it requires a master of wordes suche as my Father, for I am no more than an uncultivated miner with pick and shovell. Confident of the golde wich I must surely discover, and forgetfull of my Father's warnings, my brothers incurrd an enormous debt in the construxion of a mill at Martyrios, where they commencd the manufacture of sugar and the distillage of brandie, and therewith purchasd more slaves for this new toyl.

The first yeare a deferrment of payment was requested as the Martyrios harveste was still not suffishent *sufficient* to support the mill and indeed did not yeeld suffishentlie to pay towards the debt. My brothers pressd for all speede and dispatch in findyng the golde and theyr grate urgencie resulted in worsenyng the performance of my dutie. The second yeare gone by, the money-lender come for his cashe, presentyng statements of increasd losse and cessant revenue, all we could afforde to pay that odious man was the interest charges for two yeares; hence we were still owing for the same mill and the same slaves, as if there had been nobodie at work those two long yeares. This demonstrates how littl value worke enjoys in this countrie and tymes and indeed the great value of money in relasion; suche is the system of the Realme and of Europe which was introducd here without our being informd or consulted. And thus there followd goode yeares and bad yeares one after the othere

suche that we could not pay our debt, and my brothers began to heap
insult and humiliation upon me, aggravatyng me with suche rebuke and
reproche that I responded with immodest wordes, throwyng the letter
on the table for whoever thought they could make better use of it, tho'
this went agaynst the instruxions Father had so wisely layd out for us.

This altercation and my owne displeaure proved to take me farre
away, first from Martyrios to Sabarâ, a village of exceedyng delycious
water, and onto Villa Rica, with its bothersome prices, where I remaynd for the celebrations of the arrivall of the new Governor of
the Captaincy, the Viscount of Barbacena. *And where five days later
everyone regretted their hospitality when the young governor reminded the
inhabitants of Minas that they owed the queen one hundred stone of gold,
listing every penny of overdue taxes and all sorts of other unpleasantries.
Which led to the noblemen's conspiracy and the rest is history.* I journeyed
on to Rio de Janeyro and to Portugal, Africa, India, and Macao,
servyng in this circuit as a person of rank and responsibilitie in the
commerce of the most coveted goodes of the nations of Europe.

Thirty-one long yeares I remaynd in that occupation before re-
turnyng to Minas with great reserves of fortune and two intentions,
the first to die in Martyrios *he must be about seventy himself by now* and
the second to have done with the discoverie of Martinho Dias's golde,
if the wich had not already beene accomplished.

Of mynes there were no more, nor the Martyrios Estate, nor a single
Perdigão. Almost everythyng was ruins and desertion. The most wealth-
ie, populous and merry dystrict, which had beene Villa Rica, was to be
fownd in total dissolution, with many fewer inhabitants than had beene
before, and it was as reparation for the mistreatment that had beene
practissed. Golde was presentlie being extrakted from mines of great
deepnesse administerd by British companys with as muche machinerie
as people; to the older residents of Minas Geraes it had seemd more
convenient to go into the wildernesse and plant cane and rayse cattel,
while some with a goode nose for future businesse had planted coffee,

and it seemd to many that the end of the adventurous quests for golde
by individuals had arrived.

For me it was beginnyng all over againe. I managed to regayne owner-
shipp of Martyrios, wich had beene loste by the Perdigãos twenty-seven
years earlier, and I assayed to find *looked for* any Perdigão in the most distant settlments, circulatyng the news over speaker boxes and by towne
crier accordyng to the custome of the place, and as welle among the
poorest of people who were congregating in large multitudes at farmes
and estates in searche of any sort of service, and even at the Courte
the news was read, in the Gazette of Rio de Janeyro. (I have fayled in
this account to remarke upon the circumstances of the removal of the
Courte from Lisbon to Rio de Janeyro in the yeare 1808, being in the
business of merchante shippyng myselfe at that tyme.)

The renovation of the estate lasted two yeares, and so emmersed in
labors so demandyng was I that it was unbeknownst to me that the Kinge
of Brazil declard independence, this news reaching me muche in delay,
not allowyng for festivitys. From not one Perdigão did I receive an answer
to my calle, the wich I repeated yeare after yeare, allways finding myselfe
muche in need of that letter of Martinho Dias's and even more desyring
the friendship and companie of relations. After some yeares I learnt of the
existence of a half-wit Perdigão hidden away on an estate near the river
das Velhas, and he was in actualitie lesse of a half-wit than he seemd,
since people had mistakenlie taken for fantastic the truest things he
sayd, suche as his possessing stone after stone of hidden golde. In him I
met the son of my brother Ioão, the eldest, borne and raysed before I left
here and I believe he recognized me only dimmly; he knew nothing of
the Perdigãos and less of the letter, and came with me to Martyrios.

Thereupon took place this shockyng occurrence: in the yeare 1827,
Martinho Dias's letter was published in the Rio de Janeyro Gazette.
Holy shit. Some unschoold person who led caravans to the Courte had
fownd it insyde a bottle, hidden in a grottoe of the Piedade Mountains,
and took it to bee printed in the Gazette. *Why assume it was an illiterate?*

Seems to me that's a shaky hypothesis. Who's to say the guy didn't look for the gold first, then give up and take the letter to the newspaper? Who's to say he didn't publish it in hopes of bringing to light some new facts which might lead him to the gold, some piece of information he was missing? You've got to take it slow with hypotheses like these, lots of things could have happened before that letter ever made it to the Gazette. Considerablie taken by surprise and distresse was I at having our so ancient a secret *what bull* thus reveald, since at that tyme I judged it to be the same letter wich had beene lost with the Perdigãos. *What? And it wasn't?*

I serched the locations referred to therein as rugged and mountainous but somethyng seemd strange, however what somethyng it being impossible to know for the reason that I was unable to stimulate the memorie of the wordes which slumberd, conceeled, in my minde. *What words? What memory?* That nephew of mine unravaled *unraveled* it all; when first presst by me with questions he insisted with obstinassie on revealyng nothing, clayming not to be in possession of his senses, until it occurred to me to reade to him the aforementiond letter, and miraculouslie his eyes opened in understandyng, and he smiled and said tapa-cû, tapa-cû *Mother of God he's going to get there!* and without furthere obstinassie he went up onto the roofe and liftyng a few tyles as bats flew out all arounde he extracted a clay pot *it's the letter* which he brawt *brought* to me and repeated: tapa-cû. *It's the guy from Santa Luzia!* I broke open the pot *it's got to be him* and therein fownde the letter of our misfortune, wich upon rereading was not an exact copie of the one wich had been publishd *No!* having one and another considerable discrepancys regardyng the sites *what now?* wich causd me some perplexitie and meditation, for if I supposd that the error was innocent the consideration of the disentanglyng would be one thinge, and quite another if sayd error were mallitious. *Elementary, my dear fellow.*

The certaintie to wich I came was that it was mallitious *I think so too tho' I could not fathm Martinho Dias's motives. Same as mine? Yours?* On this supposition I assayd *tried* to reconstruct the texte, wich I did separatyng one from the other what they did not have in common *you got it* as referrd to belowe.

Transcription of the copie from the Gazette:

"in a notch facing the place the Indian sayd was called Caetê we fownd a veyne"

Transcription from the Perdigãos' copie:

"in a notch facing Ita-pucu, three leagues riding the ridge to the Easte of that place we fownd a veyne"

Fantastic. Obviously quite a calculated move, maybe even a precaution against Borba Gato himself. Now it was just a matter of fitting the two parts together, and bango. With great expectation I assayd to inmesh the two partes in the manner seemyng most certayn wich seemd to me was the followyng:

"in a notch facing Ita-pucu, three leagues riding the ridge to the Easte of that place that the Indian sayd was called Caetê, we fownd a veyne"

Of course! That changes everything. Three leagues, hmmm, six times three is eighteen, eighteen kilometers from Caetê, not from Itapucu. Of course. The terme place being thus situatd at the ende of the differyng parte in one and at the commencement of the differyng parte in the other, it seemd to me that the two ought to be joynd, ende and beginnyng, to be able to understand the middle. *Hmmm.*

Then I was right? I departed well-supplyd from Martyrios for the wildernesse and arrived in Caetê from where I passed to that group of mountains the older Indians called Itapucu and wich were not the same ones still referrd to as Ita-pucu, for the whytes corrupted the name to applie to the whole range, thus was the real Itapucu was knowne to only a few. I serched all around those ridges lookyng for some sign allong the jagged pathes, having little remayning endurance for so arduoss an enterprize, when I came to the realization that Caetê not being a towne or a village in 1699 Martinho Dias could not have giv'n it as a reference *obviously!* and thus was he probablie referryng to the border of the forrest wich is what the Indians called caatê. I moved a goode quarter league to the west and fownd the confownded golde.

For the reasons already made knowne to you *it sounds like he's sick and tired of the story—and there can't be much more to go, really, two pages or so.* He could have at least described how he felt finding the gold after so many long-suffering years. What a strange man. Dry. *Not a single detail about his work in the Orient, not a word about whether he married there, or ever had children, nothing about the Brazilian monarchs, regents, the Constitution of '24, the abdication, Republicans, Liberals, nothing. He only mentions independence in passing. A strange man to be sure. Could he have been in too much of a hurry to include more details? Or maybe he just wasn't interested?* For the reasons already made knowne to you in this commemorative, I was not able to make use of this treasure, thus it will coste me nothing to give it up, for God did not make suche for our pleasure or he would not have kept it so hidden from our eyes. These occurrences were to happen accordyng to order and as I make them knowne to you my obligation is thereby finallie met with the discoverie, tho' what worthe does this golde offer suche an agèd man? And to whom to bequeath it not having fownd a Perdigão of any use in all these yeares, and if the yeares left to my living will not be either long or kinde enough to provyde room for this difficult discoverie? The Perdigãos *they're scattered all over Brazil, poor folk working farms that could have belonged to them* were only meant to be guardians, not proprietors, of the golde, and so considerd I the destinie of my inheritance, followyng the example of the first to finde the golde, who hid it so engeniously in order that he who findes it in his time shall bee a person with the requisite of full capacitie, to be trusted in the finding as well as in the goode use of the finde, when God is servd.

It is six yeares we have annuallie reeped golde from that veyne and it has giv'n some happynesse only to my nephew, in the forme of the purchase of a house on a delitefull little hill in the charmyng village of Santa Luzia *didn't I tell you? It's him, it's him!* from whence he comes eache February to dilligentlie dig and surreptitiously carry away the stonesweight of golde upon wich he lives comfortablie for the remaynder of the yeare, and recently the poor fellow saw his worke increasd by the incomprehensible (to him) taske of going to the adjacent peake to cut a great rock and install with the utmost laboriousness and prolongd adjustments a large mirrore in the forme of a crosse *son-of-a-bitch* and then to remove it and install in those same holes a placard made by myselfe carvd in the hardest wood as it must be done, with the followyng inscription:

"Site of the discoverie of muche golde in the yeare 1699; God will make it to shine when he is served."

That is the tale I have to tell. I ask that you not take it for literature as it does not pretende to be so, because I am as muche lackyng in Grammar and Science, correctable faults, as I am in Talent, the wich has no cure, for *you don't learn to samba in school,* one is borne with it or not; nevertheless I woulde wish that you take this for a lesson and also, if it woulde do as suche, as the final entertaymnent offerd to a person who wound his waye to the ende of these diffycult speccullations.

Completed at Martyrios the 24th of Auguste of the yeare 1833.

Estevam de Saa Perdigão.

The metaphor is complete.

Pierre Albert-Birot, *Grabinoulor*.
Yuz Aleshkovsky, *Kangaroo*.
Felipe Alfau, *Chromos*.
  Locos.
  Sentimental Songs.
Ivan Ângelo, *The Celebration*.
  The Tower of Glass.
Alan Ansen, *Contact Highs: Selected Poems 1957-1987*.
David Antin, *Talking*.
Djuna Barnes, *Ladies Almanack*.
  Ryder.
John Barth, *LETTERS*.
  Sabbatical.
Andrei Bitov, *Pushkin House*.
Louis Paul Boon, *Chapel Road*.
Roger Boylan, *Killoyle*.
Ignácio de Loyola Brandão, *Zero*.
Christine Brooke-Rose, *Amalgamemnon*.
Brigid Brophy, *In Transit*.
Meredith Brosnan, *Mr. Dynamite*.
Gerald L. Bruns,
  Modern Poetry and the Idea of Language.
Gabrielle Burton, *Heartbreak Hotel*.
Michel Butor, *Mobile*.
  Portrait of the Artist as a Young Ape.
Julieta Campos, *The Fear of Losing Eurydice*.
Anne Carson, *Eros the Bittersweet*.
Camilo José Cela, *The Family of Pascual Duarte*.
  The Hive.
Louis-Ferdinand Céline, *Castle to Castle*.
  London Bridge.
  North.
  Rigadoon.
Hugo Charteris, *The Tide Is Right*.
Jerome Charyn, *The Tar Baby*.
Marc Cholodenko, *Mordechai Schamz*.
Emily Holmes Coleman, *The Shutter of Snow*.
Robert Coover, *A Night at the Movies*.
Stanley Crawford, *Some Instructions to My Wife*.
Robert Creeley, *Collected Prose*.
René Crevel, *Putting My Foot in It*.
Ralph Cusack, *Cadenza*.
Susan Daitch, *L.C.*
  Storytown.
Nigel Dennis, *Cards of Identity*.
Peter Dimock,
  A Short Rhetoric for Leaving the Family.
Ariel Dorfman, *Konfidenz*.
Coleman Dowell, *The Houses of Children*.
  Island People.
  Too Much Flesh and Jabez.
Rikki Ducornet, *The Complete Butcher's Tales*.
  The Fountains of Neptune.
  The Jade Cabinet.
  Phosphor in Dreamland.
  The Stain.
William Eastlake, *The Bamboo Bed*.
  Castle Keep.
  Lyric of the Circle Heart.
Jean Echenoz, *Chopin's Move*.
Stanley Elkin, *A Bad Man*.
  Boswell: A Modern Comedy.
  Criers and Kibitzers, Kibitzers and Criers.
  The Dick Gibson Show.
  The Franchiser.

George Mills.
The Living End.
The MacGuffin.
The Magic Kingdom.
Mrs. Ted Bliss.
The Rabbi of Lud.
Van Gogh's Room at Arles.
Annie Ernaux, *Cleaned Out*.
Lauren Fairbanks, *Muzzle Thyself*.
  Sister Carrie.
Leslie A. Fiedler,
  Love and Death in the American Novel.
Ford Madox Ford, *The March of Literature*.
Carlos Fuentes, *Terra Nostra*.
  Where the Air Is Clear.
Janice Galloway, *Foreign Parts*.
  The Trick Is to Keep Breathing.
William H. Gass, *The Tunnel*.
  Willie Masters' Lonesome Wife.
Etienne Gilson, *The Arts of the Beautiful*.
  Forms and Substances in the Arts.
C. S. Giscombe, *Giscome Road*.
  Here.
Douglas Glover, *Bad News of the Heart*.
Karen Elizabeth Gordon, *The Red Shoes*.
Patrick Grainville, *The Cave of Heaven*.
Henry Green, *Blindness*.
  Concluding.
  Doting.
  Nothing.
Jiří Gruša, *The Questionnaire*.
John Hawkes, *Whistlejacket*.
Aidan Higgins, *A Bestiary*.
  Flotsam and Jetsam.
  Langrishe, Go Down.
Aldous Huxley, *Antic Hay*.
  Crome Yellow.
  Point Counter Point.
  Those Barren Leaves.
  Time Must Have a Stop.
Mikhail Iossel and Jeff Parker, eds.,
  *Amerika: Contemporary Russians View the
  United States*.
Gert Jonke, *Geometric Regional Novel*.
Jacques Jouet, *Mountain R.*
Danilo Kiš, *Garden, Ashes*.
  A Tomb for Boris Davidovich.
Tadeusz Konwicki, *A Minor Apocalypse*.
  The Polish Complex.
Elaine Kraf, *The Princess of 72nd Street*.
Jim Krusoe, *Iceland*.
Ewa Kuryluk, *Century 21*.
Violette Leduc, *La Bâtarde*.
Deborah Levy, *Billy and Girl*.
  Pillow Talk in Europe and Other Places.
José Lezama Lima, *Paradiso*.
Osman Lins, *Avalovara*.
  The Queen of the Prisons of Greece.
Alf Mac Lochlainn, *The Corpus in the Library*.
  Out of Focus.
Ron Loewinsohn, *Magnetic Field(s)*.
D. Keith Mano, *Take Five*.
Ben Marcus, *The Age of Wire and String*.
Wallace Markfield, *Teitlebaum's Window*.
  To an Early Grave.

FOR A FULL LIST OF PUBLICATIONS, VISIT:
www.dalkeyarchive.com

SELECTED DALKEY ARCHIVE PAPERBACKS

DAVID MARKSON, *Reader's Block.*
  Springer's Progress.
  Wittgenstein's Mistress.
CAROLE MASO, *AVA.*
LADISLAV MATEJKA AND KRYSTYNA POMORSKA, EDS.,
  Readings in Russian Poetics: Formalist and Structuralist
  Views.
HARRY MATHEWS,
  The Case of the Persevering Maltese: Collected Essays.
  Cigarettes.
  The Conversions.
  The Human Country: New and Collected Stories.
  The Journalist.
  Singular Pleasures.
  The Sinking of the Odradek Stadium.
  Tlooth.
  20 Lines a Day.
ROBERT L. MCLAUGHLIN, ED.,
  Innovations: An Anthology of Modern &
  Contemporary Fiction.
STEVEN MILLHAUSER, *The Barnum Museum.*
  In the Penny Arcade.
RALPH J. MILLS, JR., *Essays on Poetry.*
OLIVE MOORE, *Spleen.*
NICHOLAS MOSLEY, *Accident.*
  Assassins.
  Catastrophe Practice.
  Children of Darkness and Light.
  The Hesperides Tree.
  Hopeful Monsters.
  Imago Bird.
  Impossible Object.
  Inventing God.
  Judith.
  Natalie Natalia.
  Serpent.
  The Uses of Slime Mould: Essays of Four Decades.
WARREN F. MOTTE, JR.,
  Fables of the Novel: French Fiction since 1990.
  Oulipo: A Primer of Potential Literature.
YVES NAVARRE, *Our Share of Time.*
WILFRIDO D. NOLLEDO, *But for the Lovers.*
FLANN O'BRIEN, *At Swim-Two-Birds.*
  At War.
  The Best of Myles.
  The Dalkey Archive.
  Further Cuttings.
  The Hard Life.
  The Poor Mouth.
  The Third Policeman.
CLAUDE OLLIER, *The Mise-en-Scène.*
FERNANDO DEL PASO, *Palinuro of Mexico.*
ROBERT PINGET, *The Inquisitory.*
RAYMOND QUENEAU, *The Last Days.*
  Odile.
  Pierrot Mon Ami.
  Saint Glinglin.
ANN QUIN, *Berg.*
  Passages.
  Three.
  Tripticks.
ISHMAEL REED, *The Free-Lance Pallbearers.*
  The Last Days of Louisiana Red.
  Reckless Eyeballing.
  The Terrible Threes.

  The Terrible Twos.
  Yellow Back Radio Broke-Down.
JULIÁN RÍOS, *Poundemonium.*
AUGUSTO ROA BASTOS, *I the Supreme.*
JACQUES ROUBAUD, *The Great Fire of London.*
  Hortense in Exile.
  Hortense Is Abducted.
  The Plurality of Worlds of Lewis.
  The Princess Hoppy.
  Some Thing Black.
LEON S. ROUDIEZ, *French Fiction Revisited.*
LUIS RAFAEL SÁNCHEZ, *Macho Camacho's Beat.*
SEVERO SARDUY, *Cobra & Maitreya.*
NATHALIE SARRAUTE, *Do You Hear Them?*
  Martereau.
ARNO SCHMIDT, *Collected Stories.*
  Nobodaddy's Children.
CHRISTINE SCHUTT, *Nightwork.*
GAIL SCOTT, *My Paris.*
JUNE AKERS SEESE,
  Is This What Other Women Feel Too?
  What Waiting Really Means.
AURELIE SHEEHAN, *Jack Kerouac Is Pregnant.*
VIKTOR SHKLOVSKY,
  A Sentimental Journey: Memoirs 1917-1922.
  Theory of Prose.
  Third Factory.
  Zoo, or Letters Not about Love.
JOSEF ŠKVORECKÝ,
  The Engineer of Human Souls.
CLAUDE SIMON, *The Invitation.*
GILBERT SORRENTINO, *Aberration of Starlight.*
  Blue Pastoral.
  Crystal Vision.
  Imaginative Qualities of Actual Things.
  Mulligan Stew.
  Pack of Lies.
  The Sky Changes.
  Something Said.
  Splendide-Hôtel.
  Steelwork.
  Under the Shadow.
W. M. SPACKMAN, *The Complete Fiction.*
GERTRUDE STEIN, *Lucy Church Amiably.*
  The Making of Americans.
  A Novel of Thank You.
PIOTR SZEWC, *Annihilation.*
ESTHER TUSQUETS, *Stranded.*
DUBRAVKA UGRESIC, *Thank You for Not Reading.*
LUISA VALENZUELA, *He Who Searches.*
BORIS VIAN, *Heartsnatcher.*
PAUL WEST, *Words for a Deaf Daughter & Gala.*
CURTIS WHITE, *Memories of My Father Watching TV.*
  Monstrous Possibility.
  Requiem.
DIANE WILLIAMS, *Excitability: Selected Stories.*
  Romancer Erector.
DOUGLAS WOOLF, *Wall to Wall.*
  Ya! & John-Juan.
PHILIP WYLIE, *Generation of Vipers.*
MARGUERITE YOUNG, *Angel in the Forest.*
  Miss MacIntosh, My Darling.
REYOUNG, *Unbabbling.*
LOUIS ZUKOFSKY, *Collected Fiction.*
SCOTT ZWIREN, *God Head.*

FOR A FULL LIST OF PUBLICATIONS, VISIT:
www.dalkeyarchive.com